Branson Hawk

U.S. Marshal

Book Three

The Beginning

Randall Dale

The Beginning

Randall Dale

This is a work of fiction. Names, characters, places, and incidents either are the product of the author's imagination or are used fictitiously. Any resemblance to actual events or persons, living or dead, is entirely coincidental.

ISBN: 9781697194623

Printed October 2019 in the

United States of America

Prologue

Dark, towering thunderclouds shrouded the top of the Rincon Mountains east of Tucson, and occasional flashes of lightning lit the darkening sky overhead. I pulled my hat and slicker tighter against the fury of the increasing wind as it rushed down the canyon. I gave my horse his head, allowing him to pick his way through the boulder-strewn creek, all the while knowing that as each step took us higher into the mountains, each step also   brought me closer to the danger that awaited there.

The man I chased had robbed a store in Tucson by beating the owner and emptying the cash box. He had stolen a horse and headed into the mountains to escape the law, but I was the law and there was no escaping me. Colonel Marcomb, the head of the U.S. Marshals in the Tucson district, had urged me to begin pursuit, and he had shown increasing frustration as I took my time gathering the few provisions and supplies I knew I would need. I packed my saddlebags, tied my slicker to the cantle and mounted. With a touch to my hat brim, I saluted the Colonel and jogged steadily to the foothills and the mountains beyond. I was an hour or more behind the man and I could have worn my horse out in a mad dash to make up ground, but with darkness approaching, I knew there would be no confrontation that night.

The peaks grew closer as my bay kept the pace. Shadows lengthened as the sun approached the horizon to my back, but I wasn't worried. I was in my element now, away from the deception I so often found in town, away from the pretended niceties and everyday interactions with townfolk, away from the young women who giggled or scoffed at my clumsiness, and away from mundane report writing or reading that took too much of a marshal's time. I was alone, doing what I did best, tracking the fugitive with only one goal, to capture and bring him to justice, for justice was the one constant in my life.

At my first opportunity, I left the dry creek bed and the danger of the inevitable flash flood. I had seen the force and devastation a wall of water could bring and I wanted no part of it. At a flat place on the ravine wall, I found a thick stand of trees and wove a tight shelter from pine boughs. I stripped my saddle and picketed my horse in a somewhat sheltered cove with plenty of grass, then I built a small fire and made coffee. I smiled to myself. The Colonel and the storeowner's wife had insisted on my leaving immediately and had grown agitated at my deliberateness, but the short time spent in preparation had been worth it, for I had coffee to drink, food to eat and a blanket to keep me warm. If I had started the journey with no forethought, I would have been as the man I tracked, hungry, cold and wet. I thought of the thief. I didn't know who he was and didn't care. By the next day I would have him in custody and on his way back to Tucson for trial. I reveled in the task. Truth be told, I loved it.

The flash flood came as no surprise and I smiled again from the safety of my camp above the water line. Darkness had come to the land so I couldn't see, but I heard the churning mass of water, boulders and trees as it crashed along the once dry creek bed. Within a minute, rain came to the lower elevations with huge, scattered, splatting raindrops that grew in intensity until nothing but the pounding of the rain could be heard. I drained the last of the coffee in my cup and chewed my fourth piece of fried beef, then rested my head against the saddle and pulled my blanket over me.

The monsoon storm passed quickly in the night and the sun's first rays of morning found a cloudless, summer sky. I rolled out of my blanket and stretched my arms high overhead. In the creek, only a trickle remained of the destructive flash flood of the night before. I shook my head in wonderment. Arizona's weather had to be the most interesting of any place in the country.

Deciding to get an early start to find the fugitive, I packed the saddlebags, only taking a hard biscuit and several pieces of jerky to eat on the way. The bay was anxious in the early morning coolness so I saddled and pointed him east. Three miles up the canyon, I found where the thief had spent the night in a grove of aspens. I grunted to myself. It had been a poorly chosen location and there had been no fire. He had spent a long, miserable night, wet, cold and likely hungry. I shook my head. Chances were good he would be happy to get caught and taken back to a dry cell.

After the rain, the horse tracks were easy to read and within the hour I could see flashes through the trees of the horse and rider ahead. The man was large with longish, black hair, a thick neck and broad shoulders. He had no hat and no coat and he rode with head down and shoulders sagging. I could plainly see he was done in and my guess was that he probably hadn't slept in the night. He made no effort to watch his back trail so I kicked my bay into a trot. In no time I rode only a few paces behind and could have ridden there unnoticed for a long time had his horse not seen us.

The long-legged sorrel stopped and turned to look at us. The man lifted his eyes and peered at me with confusion. His thick eyelids blinked heavily under dark, brushy eyebrows.

"Who are you?"

He had no weapon that I could see and I remembered that he'd beaten the store owner rather than threatening with a gun. But there was no reason to take a chance so I slowly pulled my Colt .45 and held it on my saddle horn.

"Name is Branson Hawk, U.S. Marshal. I've come to take you back to Tucson."

His eyes grew wide. "How did you find me?"

I made a face. He had probably been the easiest pursuit I'd ever undertaken. The stupidity of some outlaws was almost unbelievable. "Friend, as far as I'm concerned, you were never lost."

He quickly glanced left and right and I could see he contemplated a run for freedom. I aimed and cocked my pistol. The click was incredibly loud in the early morning stillness. He looked at the .45 pointed at him over my horse's ears. In seconds, his shoulders dropped and it was plain to see any fight he might have had was long gone. He raised his hands in surrender.

I grinned. "First smart thing you've done since you walked into that store yesterday." I rode to his side. "Cross your hands behind your back."

His surrender was complete. He obeyed without objection and with one hand holding my pistol, I used the other to press handcuffs around each of his wrists. I gathered the reins of his long-legged sorrel and turned to jog west toward town.

The afternoon summer heat of Tucson pressed against my shoulders and chest making breathing difficult, especially after coming from the higher elevations and the coolness of the pines. Men and women watched from shaded boardwalks, some pointing at us while conversing among themselves. I was sure they spoke to one another of my skills as a tracker and prowess as a superior lawman. I puffed my chest and looked straight ahead while enjoying what I was certain was unrestrained appreciation that I was willing to serve as a U.S. Marshal to keep their town safe.

I rode to the jail at the Sheriff's Office on the main street, where I flipped the sorrel's reins over the hitching rail. I glanced to the burley robber and shook my head. He had been tired on the mountain, but the long ride down to Tucson had drained every last hint of strength from him. He swayed in the saddle, then before I could steady him, he fell from the horse and landed on the ground with a grunt.

I frowned, but I wasn't overly concerned. He'd made his choice and was paying the price. I stepped from my bay, taking time to tie my reins to the rail before assisting the black-headed thief to his feet. I held him as he ascended onto the boardwalk and into the office.

Deputy Brett grinned as he stood and pulled his watch from his pocket. "I win the bet. I told the other deputies you'd be back before five o'clock."

I nodded. "What time is it?"

"A little after four."

I smirked in exaggerated self-importance. "Actually took me longer than I'd planned." I pointed to the wooden door separating the cells in the back from the office in the front. "If you'll be so kind as to unlock the door, I'll leave him in your charge." I motioned with my head toward the street. "Then I'm going to the Peacock House to wash the dust from my throat, and after that I'm heading to Lolita's eatery for at least three plates of stew."

His grin grew as he looked at me. "That's what you think. The Colonel stopped by and said he needs to see you when you got back to town. Said he would be at the courthouse until dark."

I pursed my lips and took a deep breath. He undoubtedly

had another assignment for me. It wouldn't pay to grumble, for it was the life I'd chosen. With a nod toward Brett, I led the prisoner to the back and took the handcuffs off as he entered the cell. He didn't speak, but flopped onto the bed like he'd been planning on it the entire trip.

The Peacock house called my name as I passed by on the boardwalk on my way to the courthouse. I glanced inside to see the gambling hall and saloon full to overflowing with every sort of man that inhabited Tucson. A drink would have tasted mighty good about then, but duty called so I passed by.

The Colonel sat at an oversized desk piled high with papers and folders. He stood when I entered. "Did you bring him in?"

Never once had the Colonel sent me after a man that I didn't bring in, either upright or tied over a saddle. I could have made a frivolous remark, but decided against it. The Colonel didn't always appreciate honest appraisals of my worth. "Yes, sir. He's in a cell at the Sheriff's Office."

"Good." He stepped around to half sit, half lean against the desk. He folded his arms but didn't speak.

His actions confused me. He seemed as though he wanted to tell me something but held back.

I hitched my pants to my hips. "Brett said you wanted to see me?"

"Yes, yes." He stood and pointed with his nose to the street. "Feller came in a couple of hours ago. Said he needed to see you."

"Who was he?"

Marcomb shrugged. "Didn't give a name, but there was something about him I didn't like."

"Like what?"

He brushed papers from his leaning spot and rested on the edge of the desk. "He said he was an old friend of yours from way back, but he looked awfully rough."

I tucked my thumbs into the front of my pants. More'n half the people I knew, especially those I called my friends, were what the Colonel would call rough. For certain, I was among the roughest of the lot.

"So, what are you trying to say?"

"He wants to meet you at the old, abandoned livery barn on the back side of fourth street."

"Fine. Any time in particular?"

Marcomb shook his head. "He said any time before dark."

"I'll go now." I pulled my hat tighter on my head and turned to leave.

To my surprise, he reached and hefted a gun from a rack mounted on the wall. "I'm going with you."

I cocked my head and gazed at him. "Why would you need to do that?"

"Can't rightly say. But I'd feel some better if you didn't go alone."

"Pshaww! It'll be in broad daylight." I waved my arm. "What harm could come if he's an old friend of mine?"

The desk drawer squealed in protest as the Colonel pulled it back. He reached and pulled a box out, then opened the double-barrel shotgun and pushed shells from the box into each barrel. He closed the gun with a clack and held it in the crook of his arm. "I don't mind going."

I knew he cared about each of the men who worked for him and he was a good man, as good a man as I could have hoped to have for a supervisor as well as a friend. "Colonel, I appreciate what you are doing, but honestly, it doesn't seem to me to be as dangerous as you are making it out to be. In the first place, if this mystery man was planning on ambushing me, why would he come to you and ask to give me the message?"

Marcomb made a face and tilted his head back and forth while thinking. Finally, he stopped and peered at me. "I suppose that makes sense." He replaced the scattergun to its place in the rack, then waved his hand. "Very well then, off with you."

I walked east from the courthouse toward Fourth Street and the abandoned barn. I didn't know who waited for me there. It might well have been a friend, but the other possibility definitely crossed my mind. The Colonel had been nervous and I made the decision to be ready in case the man was something different than what he claimed. I reached and slipped the thong from my pistol and loosened it from the holster. I'd be ready just in case.

The big, double doors of the barn were opened wide and tied back. I hesitated for a moment and rubbed the smooth, wooden handle of my .45. I suddenly had an uneasy feeling about entering. I didn't know who was inside and the smart thing to do would have been to wait, or better yet, have the Colonel stand next to me with his deadly scattergun. He had made the offer, should I have allowed him to walk with me?

I shook my head. I'd been in more dangerous situations many times and had come out standing. I was sure my hesitation was nothing more than a reaction to the Colonel's nervousness. On top of that, if I was to be ambushed, why would the man specifically give me notice? I smirked at my hesitation. Nothing ominous awaited me, I was certain of it. After all, I was capable, I could take care of myself. Sixteen years as a U.S. Marshal and countless arrests over the years attested to that. Besides, my skills with a six-gun were well known in Tucson and beyond. What was there to worry about?

I strode purposefully through the doors, then stopped to look around. It was vacant for the most part, with only a few empty stalls alongside one wall. I saw no one as I studied the interior of the big building, so I walked in, turning from side to side to find the man who supposedly waited for me there.

Seeing nothing, I called, "Hello."

I jumped at the sound of his voice behind me.

"Branson Hawk!"

I turned. He stood in the shadow with his hat pulled low so I couldn't see his face, a lanky man with a confident, arrogant posture. He took one step toward the light. My eyes opened wide as I recognized the man. It was a face I'd seen only twice before and hoped I'd never see again. A face with a sinister, humorless smile that haunted my dreams. A pockmarked face of a killer worse than any I'd known.

He silently taunted me, watching unconcerned with purposeful inaction as my hand flashed to the gun in my holster. His nonchalant waiting was the most troubling and in that spec of an instant, I knew fear. It was as though he knew he had nothing to worry about and he mocked me, giving me the chance to draw first. When he finally moved, it was with such swiftness that my .45 had not cleared leather when I saw the flash of his gun and at the same moment, felt the bullet enter my chest. I cursed my stupidity and my pride. Compared to him, my movements had been slow and clumsy, and I realized too late that although I was good, I should have worked at being better.

The impact jolted me and my right hand went straightaway numb. I tried to hold the .45, tried to stand to defend myself, but my pistol fell to the dirt as I sank to my knees.

He unhurriedly approached, then knelt and held the front of my shirt with his four-fingered left hand to keep me from falling. His right hand pointed his pistol into my left eye and he leaned to my ear. "So, Branson Hawk, we meet again. I've remembered you for the past fifteen years in the Missouri State Prison. Do you remember?"

Remember? Yes I did remember. I blinked my unencumbered eye heavily, then realized I couldn't hold it open any longer. In that instant I was overwhelmed with thoughts of Kansas.

Randall Dale

Chapter 1

Lawrence Kansas, December, 1859

The cold wind over the prairie whistled through the short, squat dugout cabin. I swear, there were more holes in the walls than in my hand-me-down coveralls, and there were plenty in them. I could hear my ma rattling pots and pans next to the wood-burning stove on the other side of the thin wall, and it was my job to bring in the wood and buffalo chips for the fire. I flipped my moth-eaten wool blanket and rolled up from the cornhusks that made my bed on the floor, stepped over Caleb, my sleeping, seven-year-old brother and slipped my coveralls over one bare, bony shoulder. I leaned to pull a pair of oversized and over-worn hand-me-down boots onto my sockless feet before shuffling into the main room of the three-room cabin.

"Morning, ma."

She turned and smiled. That's one thing I remember. She always smiled, no matter how tough times were, and times were plenty tough. We lived on a windswept, Kansas homestead that was too cold in the winter, too hot in the summer, too dry in the spring and too wet in the fall.

"Good morning, Branson. Can you bring in a couple of extra armloads of wood this morning? It's going to be cold again today."

"Sure, Ma." I thought that the past two weeks had been bitter cold, so why would that day be any different?

I reached for my coat on a nail by the door. It wasn't mine alone, for Caleb and I shared it depending on who was outside at any given time. As I pulled the coat to my shoulders, I noticed that Pa's coat was gone.

"Ma?"

"Yes, Son."

"Where's Pa?"

Her smile faltered for only an instant, then she regained her pleasant expression and brushed imaginary wrinkles from her thin, worn, gingham dress. "He's gone to the marsh to check his traps."

She hadn't quite figured out that my ten-year-old mind could understand that he had no traps at the marsh or anywhere else. When she said he was at the marsh, it really meant that he was standing on a small hill at the edge or our homestead staring into the distance. More than a year before, my brother and I followed him. We had heard about his traps and wanted to see. We hid in a clump of sage and watched for a long time, but all he did was stand with bent head and sagging shoulders. When he finally turned to walk toward the cabin, he saw us and threatened to whip us with a switch if we ever followed him again. We ran all the way home and hid at the back of the cabin.

My pa wasn't a mean man, at least he didn't hit any of us, although he was excessively stern and had little patience with the four of us young'uns, me, Caleb, Josiah and Myrtle. If not for my ma, there would never have been any laughter in our little cabin.

I nodded to her while pulling the coat onto my shoulders. With a deep breath for courage, I opened the door and stepped into the biting wind and onto the packed earth. Pulling my coat closer with one hand, I used the other to close the door to keep some of the warmth inside.

The woodpile was at the side of the cabin under a makeshift, relatively ineffective lean-to with a slatted, board roof. With a sigh of despair, I realized the small pile would soon need replenished. My excursions into the prairie to find wood had become more difficult because everything within a close proximity to the house had been used. I shivered before wrapping my arms around as many sticks as I could carry and trudged to the door. I kicked the bottom with my boot then waited for Ma to open it and let me in.

I let the sticks fall to the hard-packed dirt floor beside the wood stove and stood for a return trip. I looked up into Ma's face. "The pile is getting mighty low. I'll need to go out gathering today."

She breathed out heavily and forced a smile. "You're a good boy, Branson. I'm sorry that life on the prairie is forcing you to grow up too fast." She swallowed, then turned abruptly to busy herself at the stove.

I shook my head. I didn't mind helping out. I would have done whatever she asked because I loved her more than anything in the world. I turned again to the door, but stopped as I reached for the corded handle. I peered over my shoulder to see her. She must have felt my eyes, for she turned and graced me with a nod and a smile, but I saw the glistening in her eyes. I hurried through the door, suddenly embarrassed. As I thought of her and her love for me, the wind, so cold and harsh at the first load of wood, seemed much less severe, and the sun, winking at me over the eastern horizon, brought the hope of better things to come.

After depositing the third armload of wood, I sat at our rough plank table while Ma, standing behind, slid a bowl of cooked mush between my elbows. She touched my shoulder. "Sorry there is no milk or molasses."

I shrugged. I hadn't expected any. Our last crop had been so poor that Pa had to sell our milk cow to pay the bill at the store. At the time, in my boyish thoughts, I was happy that I would no longer have to go out and milk every night and morning, but that happiness had long since faded at the realization that plain mush with no milk got old in a hurry.

"That's all right. I like it like this." I looked down into the bowl and forced a large spoonful of the boiled grain into my mouth so she wouldn't see my frown.

The mush gritted against my teeth as I chewed and I silently longed for meat, any kind of meat. In winters past, Pa had been able to hunt and bring in squirrels or rabbits and even an occasional deer, but six months earlier he'd taken the old musket to hunt and came back mad and empty-handed. When Ma asked what the matter was, he showed us the split barrel on the old gun. Since then we hadn't been able to afford to fix it and certainly couldn't manage a new one.

Ma rubbed my shoulder again, then adjusted her apron and stepped to the adjacent room. "Caleb, get up. It's time for breakfast."

There was no answer.

"Caleb? Are you awake?"

He groaned. "It's too cold."

I turned on the bench to see her with hands on hips and head down in weighted sorrow. "If you'll get up, I'll let you wear my sweater. Come quick while I get the twins."

I heard rustling of the cornhusks and out of the corner of my eye, watched Ma walk through the main room and lean into the bigger bedroom where she and Pa and the twins slept. In a moment she came out carrying Myrtle while leading Josiah by the hand. Both had squinted eyes at the light shining through the one glass window in the cabin. She placed Myrtle on my lap and Josiah on hers on the other side of the table.

Caleb strolled in, barefoot and bare-chested, with his overalls buttoned over one shoulder. His arms were wrapped tightly around his chest and he shivered in the cold. Ma silently removed her sweater and passed it over. Caleb quickly shoved his arms in and pulled it close.

I studied her, then with one hand holding Myrtle, I tried to shake the coat from my shoulder so she could wear it. She saw me and shook her head while mouthing the words, "I'm all right."

Caleb sat heavily next to me as he buttoned the sweater. "Thanks, Ma." He looked at the table at a bowl of mush she'd already dished out. "Not mush again."

She touched his shoulder. "Your pa promised to go help the Grunwalds. When he gets paid, he'll buy a side of bacon."

I licked my lips at the thought of bacon, but just a quickly frowned in silence. Ma's statement about the work and the bacon were nothing more than an attempt at a temporary reprieve for the younger kids. The Grunwalds were rich folks not too many miles away, and in their kindness at our meager existence, they'd offered to hire Pa for odd jobs. Ma had encouraged, even begged him to go, but he refused. I had been listening through the wall that night. Pa slapped the table and raised his voice. He said he wasn't a charity case and that he had plenty to do at the farm and didn't have time to go traipsing all over the country helping folks too lazy to do their own work. With a frown, I realized that was Pa's way. Proud to a fault, but not willing to do what needed to be done at the farm to make it successful.

I stared into my bowl while holding my sister. We shared my spoon with alternating bites of the gritty cereal, one for her then one for me. After only four bites, she shook her head and refused to eat any more. I knew how she felt, but I was old enough to know that the less I ate for breakfast, the hungrier I would be for the rest of the morning.

I finished the mush and let Myrtle down onto the dirt floor. Unlike Josiah, she had not yet learned to walk, but she could stand, provided she held to the bench. Her face screwed up in a cry, but there was nothing I could do. She was hungry for a meal, a decent meal other than boiled wheat and rye. I combed the curly locks of blonde hair out of her eyes with my fingers, then stood with a deep breath.

"Ma, I'll take the mule to gather wood. I'll be back sometime this afternoon."

She smiled sadly, then reached to tug at the lapels of my coat to pull it more closely around my chest. She looked down into my eyes and I saw again the glistening of tears in hers.

She blinked quickly then reached to gather Myrtle from the floor. She refused to look at me. "I appreciate that. You be careful."

I glanced at Caleb. "You take care of things until Pa gets back. Hear?"

"I can go with you to help."

I shook my head. "Not today. I'll have to travel a far piece to find anything worth bringing back. You would freeze to death in that sweater."

He nodded with a frown and wrapped his arms around his chest, my mention of freezing reminding him of how cold it was in the dugout. I walked out the door and looked east, toward the hill my Pa called the marsh. I gritted my teeth. Couldn't he see there was work to be done and standing on a hill wishing he was someplace else didn't make the work go away. I cocked my head. In spite of the wind whistling over the top of the sod roof of the cabin, I could hear two babies screaming and my Ma trying to comfort both. I hadn't wanted to deceive her, but I wasn't going to collect wood that day.

Our thin, flop-eared mule looked forlornly at me as I

approached the pole corral and small, adobe shelter. It wasn't much, but it kept the snow and rain off his back. I frowned when I realized he hadn't been fed that morning. I caught him with a halter and let him out of the pen to the back of the shelter where a rough-cut wooden door led to our corncrib. I opened the door, disgusted to see the sparse amount of corn. It was all we had to show for the previous summer's work. I plucked two ears of dried corn and shelled them into a pan for the mule to eat. When I got to my destination, he could graze while I did my business.

He finished eating and looked at me with the same expression Myrtle had used in the house after breakfast. He seemed to be asking if that was all he would get.

I rubbed his forehead. "Sorry, Jackson. We'll stop at the spring and let you graze the weeds there." He leaned his head against my chest while I exchanged the halter for a bridle, then I led him to the corral and climbed the pole to slip onto his back. My bony legs gripped his sides and he dropped his head in resignation, then at my urging, ambled west.

True to my promise, we stopped at the spring an hour later. Two trees made a windbreak that I stood behind while the mule grazed on the weeds and grass. He was far from finished when I nudged him to a low spot and jumped on. As before, he dropped his head and forlornly continued west.

Less than an hour later we topped a small rise and I could see the house belonging to the Grunwalds. It wasn't as large as I had expected since Ma had said they were rich. I didn't learn until later that rich simply meant anyone who had more than we did, but the house seemed to be comfortable and well cared for. I looked around for the expected servants or workers and was surprised that I could see none. I kicked the mule into a faster pace. I didn't want Mr. Grunwald to think I was a slacker. I rode Jackson to a patch of dried grass and weeds close to a large barn. When I dismounted, I hobbled his front legs to allow him graze there and not run away. I stood and patted his shoulder while looking over his back at the house. I swallowed, suddenly nervous, but with all the boldness I could muster, I walked through the garden area to the front door. I knocked and could hear action inside.

Directly, the door opened and a plump Mrs. Grunwald stared down at me in confusion. "Yes?"

"Morning, Mrs. Grunwald, ma'am. I'm Branson Hawk from east of here." I pointed over my shoulder. "You once asked my pa if he would work for you. He's too busy but I was wondering if you might consider letting me help around your place."

She took a moment to look me over from head to toe. I'm sure she wasn't impressed. I was small and thin. My too-long hair hung into my eyes, my coat and coveralls were worn. Added to that, the big boots on my feet made me look clumsy. I averted my eyes in shame.

She was silent for a long moment before reaching and grasping my chin in her soft hand. She gently pulled my face and I looked into her eyes. To my surprise, she smiled.

"Branson Hawk. How old are you?"

Ten sounded too young, no one would blame me if I fibbed a little. "Eleven-years-old, ma'am."

She nodded and looked at me suspiciously with a cockeyed glance. "Eleven?"

I dropped my head. "Coming eleven. My birthday will be in the spring."

Her eyes gleamed. "That sounds more like it." She brought her hand to her cheek in thought. "Let's see, Mr. Grunwald usually does all the hiring around here, but he's gone to town and won't be back until later."

My shoulders sagged. I'd ridden Old Jackson pert near eight miles in the cold and would be sent away for no other reason than the man of the house was gone to town. My trip had been in vain and all I had to look forward to was a long, cold return trip. I looked up to acknowledge my understanding when a sudden, harsh gust of wind pushed at my back and I took an involuntary step toward her to keep my balance. Her eyes opened wide and she pulled the door completely open and beckoned me inside.

"Glory be. Pardon my ill manners. Come in out of the cold."

I stepped in and stared at the luxury. A large fire burned brightly, invitingly, in the fireplace. I could feel the warmth on my face and I longed to stand close to smother the chill in my chest.

The woman stepped to my front and held her hand. "I'll take your coat."

I swallowed, not anxious for her to see my ragged coveralls over bare shoulders. I wished I hadn't come. "That's all right, ma'am. I shouldn't have bothered you." I turned toward the door. "I'll be on my way."

She stood between me and the door and made no effort to move. "Nonsense. You've come to work and I've got lot for you to do."

I blinked. "Are you sure."

"Sure as I'm standing here." She held her hand out again. "Now give me your coat, then you go stand by the fire to warm up."

Having no other option, I unbuttoned the only two buttons that remained on the old coat and slipped it off my shoulders. She pursed her lips as she took it, then, with a tilt of her head, she pointed to the fireplace.

"Stand there and warm up a bit."

I did and it felt mighty good. That old, hard cold had dived deep into my bones and it took a good five minutes to drive it out. While I stood there, she stepped into another room, only coming out occasionally to check on me.

In due time she approached and motioned with her head.

"Follow me."

I had difficulty keeping pace with her as she walked through the house because there was so much to gawk at. I marveled at the smooth wood floor covered at intervals with thick, woven rugs. There were couches, chairs and tables along with odds and ends on the walls. So that is what it meant to be rich? She stopped at the door at the back of the house. From a peg she pulled a flannel work shirt and handed it to me.

"Put this on. It may be a might big, but it will cover your shoulders."

I slipped into the shirt and pulled it around my chest. It was too far too big, hanging on my shoulders like an oversized tent. I buttoned it and rolled up the sleeves.

She contemplated me with a grin, then handed me my coat. "Put this back on and we'll find Curley."

I wondered who Curley was as I slipped onto my coat and buttoned both buttons. She watched for a moment before reaching for a blue, wool coat which, without putting her arms in the sleeves, she pulled around her shoulders. She grasped the door handle, pulled and stepped onto a covered porch. She put her hands to her mouth and yoo hoo'd loudly.

Someone returned the call. She looked at me with a pleased expression. "That'll be Curley. He's our hired man. He'll find a job for you."

In less than a minute, a thick black man with white hair and scraggly white beard came around the corner of one of the outbuildings. He peered at me as he approached, then turned his attention to the woman.

"Yes'm?"

"Curley, this here is Branson Hawk. You've been complaining about too much work to do and he is here to help."

He studied me up and down. "You is here to work is you?"

I looked at the woman. The man's shoulders were so broad and he appeared so menacing that I was afraid. She nodded permission to answer.

I swallowed hard as I looked up into his scowling face. "I am. I can do pert near anything." It was a lie. There was so much I didn't know how to do. I could harness a mule and help my Pa plow a field, I could gather wood and shovel mud to make sod bricks, but other than that, my skills were limited.

He nodded and his face softened. "That's good. How you be with an axe?"

"Good. My pa says I'm the best wood chopper he's ever seen." It was another lie. We owned a rusty, old axe with a broken handle. I had used it on occasion when one of the sticks I gathered was too big to fit into the stove, but I was far from proficient.

Curley nodded and looked at the woman. "Reckon he could split some wood for your fireplace?"

She smirked. "Now, Curley. I wasn't born yesterday. You know that's your job and ain't nobody going to do it for you, especially not a ten, ah, eleven-year-old boy." She put her fists on her hips. "I was thinking more along the lines of brushing the horses in the barn."

Curley looked from her to me and nodded knowingly with a huge, amused grin. His face, so frightening only a few seconds earlier, became the picture of happiness and good will. "Yes'm." He took off his hat and held it to his chest as he bowed slightly. "Can't be blaming a man for trying." He slapped his hat on his thigh and chuckled before looking at me again. "Brushing the horses and mules be a good job for a youngster who be willing to work."

She smiled with a gleam in her eye and patted my shoulder. "You go on with Curley. He'll get you started."

Randall Dale

Chapter 2

The huge, plank-sided barn was like nothing I'd ever seen. I looked at the walls with boards fit tight and any spaces filled with oakum to keep the wind out. The animals here had a better place to live than my family did. There were six closed, covered stalls on either side of a wide alley making a total of twelve. Seven had either draft horses or mules inside, and the rest appeared to be reserved for the smaller riding or buggy horses. The animals stood and watched us with heads protruding from the half doors. Curley stepped to the first of the draft horses, caught him and led him to a post in the center of the barn. He rubbed the big horse's ears, then grabbed a curry comb and brush from a shelf.

"Here you go." He pointed toward the stalls. "When you be finished with this one, you can catch the next all the way down the line." He waved his arm then grinned before turning and walking toward the double doors while singing a sorrowful tune.

I watched him retreat. Black men weren't common

around our parts. I'd only seen a handful in my entire life and the last I'd seen were a small group of thin, frowning blacks chained to the bed of a wagon. We had been on our way to town to buy supplies after selling our meager harvest. As our wagons passed on the road, they looked at us with sad and scared faces. We watched in silence and when I asked Ma who they were and why they were chained, she explained they were likely runaway slaves being taken back their owners. That was my first glimpse of slavery up close and personal. I'll never forget the sight

Ma and Pa sat in the front of the wagon talking about what we'd seen. I stood to lean over so I could hear. Pa looked up at me, then explained so I could understand, that Kansas had only recently been admitted to the union and was a free state. He told of the sacking and burning of the town of Lawrence only a few years earlier by pro-slavery men because folks in the town were outwardly abolitionists. After that raid, the area around Lawrence was among the most violent in the state as outlaws from each side had taken advantage of the feelings to rob, plunder and steal in the name of whichever side they supported.

I stood to look back to the wagon we'd passed. "But if Kansas is a free state, why are there slaves in that wagon?"

Pa sighed. "Agreements are understood that if a runaway is caught in Kansas, they can be taken back to where they belong. In fact, a feller can be arrested for helping a runaway slave."

Ma dabbed at her eyes then looked over her shoulder to the retreating wagon. I recall her deep breath and sigh. "There's going to be a war."

I shook my head at the remembrance and looked toward the black man. He took a final glance and waved at me as he closed the doors. The big barn blocked the wind and as I got busy with the brushing, I completely forgot the cold. I turned to the feather-legged draft horse and patted him hard between his front legs. He was a beautiful animal, heavily muscled and well cared for, all in direct opposition to Jackson, my flop-eared mule standing outside. I used the brush and comb to remove any dust or mud, standing on my tiptoes and stretching to reach the big horse's withers. I took my time, making sure I did a good job because I wanted Mrs. Grunwald to be more than happy with my work.

Curley returned in an hour. I was working on the fourth horse and the man seemed to be impressed. He leaned over the half-doors of the stalls, one at a time, to see the horses I'd already brushed. He nodded approvingly, then stepped closer to lean on the big sorrel's ribs.

He looked down at me and scratched the white hair at the side of his head. "You do fine work."

The statement embarrassed me. I'd never been praised by a man, including my Pa. Of course, my Ma had bragged on me, telling me what a good boy I was and how hard a worker I was, but I had never heard those words from Pa or any other grown man. I leaned down and vigorously brushed the thick legs so Curley couldn't see my face.

He continued to lean against the sorrel, quiet and still, apparently in thought. When I finished one leg and got ready to move to the other, he touched my shoulder.

"You hungry?"

I glanced into his grinning face, drawn to the man for some reason beyond my boyhood understanding. He was big and strong and somehow I felt safe when he was close. I hitched my pants to my hips. I was long past hungry, but didn't want him to know that. Ma would never show her face in town again if it was known I'd gone to the neighbor's place to get something to eat.

"No, sir."

He rubbed the big horse between his eyes. "Well, I is. Come with me."

I replaced the brush and comb to a shelf and followed

Curley out the door toward the house. Before we got to the back door, he veered to the right, down a corridor to a path leading to a heavy door built into the ground. He pulled it open with a grunt and let it fall to slam against the dirt on the side. A brief dust cloud quickly dissipated in the ever-present breeze. With a quick glance at me, he bent low and descended the earthen steps into a spacious root cellar. Toward the bottom, he turned and bade me follow.

Shelves on each side of the cutaway room held bottle after bottle of canned fruit and vegetables, but what held my attention were the sides of smoked bacon hanging from the rafters. Curley absently patted them as he leaned and scooted by. When he got to the back wall, he sat on a stool and motioned for me to sit on an identical one. A good stream of light flowed in from the open door, and the room was surprisingly comfortable with no wind and a constant temperature. He gazed at me with an expression of expectancy, then, from a shelf, he took a clear bottle and with a flourish, popped off the thin, round lid. He handed the bottle to me along with a fork from the same shelf. Then he pulled another bottle and did the same for himself.

My eyes opened wide. I'd eaten canned peaches only once before that I could recall. I licked my lips in hope while I held the bottle, unsure of what I should do. It was a full bottle, enough for my whole family. Surely he didn't expect me to eat the entire thing? I could, of course, but it would be so wasteful to eat it all in one sitting. After watching me for a moment, he grinned and motioned with his nose.

"Go on, eat up." He plunged the fork into his bottle and pulled out a large chunk of peach which he indelicately slurped into his mouth. He chewed, then turned the bottle up and drank a portion of the juice.

At his bidding, I stabbed a piece of the fruit and crammed it into my mouth. Peaches were as delicious as I had remembered. For the next five minutes we ate the incredible fruit and drank the sugary juice. I matched him bite for bite, deciding that I would quit when he did, but halfway through the jar, my stomach could hold no more. He, on the other hand, didn't stop. He ate the last remnant and turned the bottle up to swallow the remaining juice. He looked at me and grinned as he took my bottle and replaced the lid.

"How about we save this for later?"

I smiled, then wiped my mouth with the sleeve of my coat and patted my full belly. "Thank you."

He stood with a friendly grin and pointed to the opening from which the light flooded into the cellar. "I reckon we'd best get back to them hosses."

Three hours later, I turned the last horse into his stall. I'd done a good morning's work and I was proud of it. No one would have been able to brush the horses any cleaner. I hadn't seen Curley since the peaches, so after removing the halter from the classy bay riding horse, I took a moment to lean against a post with arms folded and ankles crossed. From my position I could see the loft of the barn filled to overflowing with prairie hay and a large grain crib piled high with corn ears. I shook my head at the stark comparison between our place and theirs.

"All done?"

I jerked in surprise, then turned quickly to see Curley grinning at me. He led a fine-looking, saddled gray.

"Mr. Grunwald just now rode in from town. Can you brush one more?"

"Yes, sir."

He stripped the saddle and grabbed another brush. With him on one side and me on the other, we finished and turned the horse into the last stall.

He nodded. "Good work, but now it's time for lunch." He turned and waved over his shoulder. "Come on."

I followed him to the back of the house, but this time we

didn't turn to the root cellar path but went directly to a hand pump next to the back door. He worked the handle with long, smooth strokes and water immediately poured from the spout.

"Wash up."

I pulled my coat and flannel shirtsleeves to my elbows and cupped my hands under the icy water, I washed my face, neck and hands, then stepped back. He stopped pumping and moved to the spout, then grinned. I realized he wanted me to pump for him. I jumped to the handle and jerked it up and down, happy to see an intermittent stream of water.

He washed his face, then stood and wiped his oversized hands on his pants. He pointed to the pump handle. "Smooth. You should be smooth in everything you do." He reached for the bar to push and pull using long, even strokes. "See the difference? Smooth." He stepped back. "Now you try."

I grasped the handle again, anxious to show him what I could do, but after only a few, jerky motions on my part, he shook his head.

"Slow and steady."

I slowed down, forcing the handle all the way up then all the way down.

He smiled. "That's better. In almost everything you do, slow and steady wins the race."

My puzzled expression caused him to chuckle. "Ain't you ever heard the story of the tortoise and the hare?"

My eyes opened in sudden understanding. "Yes, sir. I see what you mean now."

He patted my shoulder, then turned to the door and knocked.

"Mrs. Grunwald? I've brung the boy."

The door opened almost immediately. She smiled while wiping her hands on an apron. "So you have." She looked at me. "Are you hungry young man?" Without waiting for an answer, she hurried into the house.

I stood, waiting, unsure of what to do. Curley pushed me gently from behind.

"Hang your coat on the pegs." He pointed to the side of the door. "Then follow her."

I stepped across the threshold and did as asked. She waited for a moment before turning down a hallway. I followed to a room with a long table. As I entered, she pulled a fancy chair with carved inlays.

"Sit here."

I turned, surprised that Curley hadn't entered the house along with me. He seemed to have disappeared. I sat with my hands clasped on my lap, afraid to touch anything so fine. Unlike the table at our place, this table was polished and shiny, and rather than rough benches, it was surrounded with the nice chairs. Fine china and polished silverware sat at each place along with white, cloth napkins.

I heard footsteps and looked up, expecting to see Curley, but another man, short, round and florid faced, entered and took the chair opposite me. He shook the napkin with a pop before tucking it above the top button of his shirt. It was all foreign to me. I could only assume the new man was Mr. Grunwald. I mimicked him, hoping to look less the uncouth prairie homesteader than I actually was.

He looked at me with a cock of his head. "So you are one of the Hawk boys from east of here?"

"Yes, sir."

"And you came today to work?"

"Yes, sir."

"Henrietta says you brushed the horses?"

"I did. Finished up only a few minutes ago."

"Glad you are here to help. Old Curley isn't as spry as he used to be so some of his chores don't get done like they should. If your pa will let you, would you like to come once a week to help out?"

Randall Dale

Chapter 3

I hadn't expected a job offer and I didn't know if the man needed the help or if he was offering out of generosity. Curley hadn't seemed to me to be anything other than competent in everything he did. He was big and strong and although his hair was white, he didn't seem old.

My sole purpose for coming that day had been to get enough to buy bacon for Ma and the kids, and I'd lied about my destination. I felt ashamed of that, but hoped I'd be forgiven when I handed over the money. I swallowed and looked into the man's fat face with bushy eyebrows and bushier, mutton-chop sideburns. If he was sincere in his offer, perhaps I could come and work part of the year. We were too busy in spring, summer and fall trying to plant, grow and harvest our crops, but my biggest chores in the winter had to do with gathering firewood.

I rubbed the varnished tabletop. "I'll talk to Pa and see if I can come during the winter."

He grunted his approval, then we both turned as Mrs. Grunwald brought a large bowl to the table and ladled a generous helping into my bowl. It smelled heavenly and I had to refrain from attacking it with the silver spoon. The peaches were gone from my belly and I had worked up an appetite brushing the horses. She served her husband, then herself before taking a chair. They held hands while Mr. Grunwald said grace, then each dipped their spoons and started eating. Following their lead, I did the same, forcing myself to keep to their pace even though I wanted to devour the wonderful meal like a hungry coyote.

Mr. Grunwald wiped his mouth with the napkin. "Delicious chicken and dumplings my dear."

She smiled. "Thank you my love." She took another spoonful and looked at me.

I patted my mouth like I'd seen Mr. Grunwald do. "Yes, ma'am. I've never eaten anything so tasty." It was the truth. Ma was a passable cook. Trouble was that of late, she seldom had anything other than grains to cook.

We each finished about the same time. Mr. Grunwald pushed his bowl toward the center of the table, so I did the same.

Mrs. Grunwald frowned. "I don't think so, young man." She stood and slid the large bowl closer. "You aren't getting up from my table with only one bowl of soup in your belly." She sounded angry, but her eyes glinted and I knew she wasn't.

I suppose my eyes gleamed at the chance to eat another helping. I clumsily dipped the ladle and emptied it into my bowl.

She stood straight with her fists on her ample hips and a scowl on her face. "Come now, Branson. You can do better than that."

I swallowed, thinking that perhaps I'd read her wrong. She seemed put out about something. I looked from her to him and saw the grin. Mr. Grunwald glanced at his wife and started laughing. To my relief, she joined in.

"Eat all you want, boy." Mr. Grunwald guffawed and slapped the table.

Mrs. Grunwald sat heavily in her chair and her whole body shook as she laughed. I did the only thing I could, I emptied two more ladles into my bowl and ate with delight.

I leaned back from my empty bowl and rubbed my hands on my belly. Never in my life had I had such a delicious meal and I wished that somehow I could take some home to my family. I felt guilty that I had eaten so much while they likely had another bowl of boiled grain for lunch.

I glanced into the amused faces of the man and wife who'd treated me so well. Ma had said they were good folks, kind and generous, and I was glad for a chance to sit at their table. They peered at me, neither speaking, but their smiles expanded. I didn't know what to do and grew uncomfortable at their scrutiny. The chair squeaked as it slid back while I stood.

"I'd best be getting back home. I appreciate your letting me come work." I waited uncomfortably. I expected to get paid but didn't know how to approach the subject. I looked from the man to the woman. "Unless, of course, you have something else you'd like for me to do."

Mr. Grunwald stood and pushed his chair under the table, then with hands resting on the chair-back, he leaned while he studied me. "What do you think, my dear?" He never took his eyes from me as he asked his wife the question, but the gaze was not uncomfortable.

I glanced at her. She smiled with a nod of her head. "I'm thinking we need to pay the boy so he can get home to do his chores.

The man walked around the table while reaching into his pocket. When he got to me, he laid two silver quarters on the shiny table and pushed them closer. I stared at the money. A whole fifty cents? I'd only worked a few hours and was being paid a half dollar? I swallowed as I looked up into Mr.

Grunwald's eyes. Was this a test? I thought of all I could buy with two quarters, then I thought of Ma and our last trip to town a couple of months earlier, the one where we'd seen the slaves. Her bill had come to two dollars and change and that was supposed to be enough to see us through the winter. She had counted out the money from her small, homemade purse, gripping each coin before letting it drop to the counter.

As much as I wanted the money, I knew Ma would be disappointed if I accepted so much pay for the small amount of work. I nervously cleared my throat. "I only brushed the horses. Fifty cents is too much."

A huge grin appeared on Mr. Grunwald's face and he looked away from me to his wife. "Did you hear that Henrietta?" He patted me on my back. "I like this boy."

I gawked at him, still uncertain as to what I should do. Part of me wanted to grab the coins and run to my mule before he could change his mind, but the other part of me won out, so I waited.

He reached for the quarters and I immediately panicked. Was he taking them back? I silently cursed my stupidity. I should have taken the money with a thank you, but now he held the coins in his fat hands, slowly clinking them together by flipping the top quarter over with his thumb and tucking it behind. He repeated the process over and over. I swallowed a let out a breath, hoping for at least one of the quarters.

My disappointment was complete when he let both coins fall back into his pocket. I grimaced at my senselessness and with slumped shoulders, turned to leave.

He reached to grasp my neck. "Where you headed?"

"Home, sir."

Using his grip, he turned me toward his wife. "What do you think, Mrs. Grunwald? Did this young man come to work or not?"

"He did."

"And did you agree on a wage?"

"No, we didn't."

"I see." He gently pushed me to stand in front of him. He leaned down to look me in the eye. "Why did you come to work?"

My lip trembled. I felt so foolish. Pa had warned me that people were only out to get something for nothing. I should have listened to him. I could see now that Ma was mistaken in her high opinion of our neighbors. I looked down at my oversized boots, anxious for a chance to get away, to jump on Jackson and head for home. My shoulders seemed to press against my chest, I could barely breathe and my bottom lip, of its own accord, pushed out and curled down as I gritted my teeth. I blinked back the tears of anger, frustration, fear and regret.

The man reached and lifted my face with a hand on my chin. "What were you going to buy with your earnings?"

I pulled at my bottom lip with my teeth. His teasing may have been fun for him, but it was torture for me. I wanted to bolt for the door and never come back. My breath came in halting gasps. "Bacon, sir."

"Bacon?"

I coughed. "Yes, sir. We've ate nothing but boiled grain for pert near the whole winter. I wanted to buy some bacon for my Ma." A deep sigh, almost a wail, built in my chest and escaped even though I tried to hold it. I felt my cheeks flush with embarrassment and I tried to run, but the man held my shoulder firmly.

"Hold on, young man." He grasped my other shoulder with his free hand and pulled me to face him as he leaned again to my eye level.

To my surprise, he gently combed my hair away from my brow. I looked into his eyes and was surprised that they didn't show any mockery or any glee at my discomfort, rather, they held concern. I wiped my eyes with the sleeve of the flannel shirt, his shirt. He stood and released his hold with a comforting squeeze. I swallowed, wondering if I'd misjudged the man.

He leaned back, folding his arms while half sitting on the table next to where my bowl rested. As before, he looked at me while addressing his wife. "Henrietta, since he isn't too tickled about the idea of accepting money for his work, do we have a side of bacon we could send home with this boy?"

"Of course we do."

He tilted his head as he gazed at me. "How about it, Branson Hawk? Will you take some bacon home to your ma?"

I glanced from one to the other, unsure of what was happening. Only a moment earlier I was certain he was toying with me with every intention of keeping any money he might have been willing to pay, but now it seemed the opposite. Perhaps my Ma had been correct and my Pa mistaken. Maybe these were generous folks after all. I stood taller. "Yes, sir."

The mutton chop sideburns stood on Mr. Grunwald's face as he grinned. He looked like an oversized chipmunk. He stood from the table and motioned for me to follow him. We left the house and stepped directly to the root cellar where Curley and I had shared peaches only a few hours earlier. He threw the door open and an identical dust cloud swirled until the wind swept it away. With a quick glimpse over his shoulder, Mr. Grunwald stomped down the steps and returned in seconds carrying the bacon under his arm.

He leaned down to lift the door and let it fall closed. After it landed with a slam, he stood and yelled loud enough to raise the dead. "Curley."

In a few seconds, Curley stood in front of the man, erect, with shoulders back and his floppy hat in his hands. He looked down to his employer. "Yassir."

"Do you have a gunny sack to put this bacon in so Mr. Hawk, here, can get it home?"

"Yassir. Be right back."

Old Jackson, after grazing on the grass and weeds for much of the day, swiveled his ears and looked at me with a resigned expression. I untied the hobble rope and led him to a depression so I could jump and shimmy, belly first, onto his back. Curley grinned as he passed me the bacon. I balanced the ten-pound bundle on the mule's withers and nodded to the white-haired man.

He patted my leg. "I is glad you come by today. The Grunwalds is good folks. You come a running when you need anything and they'll hep you."

"Thank you, Curley, and tell Mr. and Mrs. Grunwald thanks again too."

His grin expanded. "I thinks that you telling them at least twenty times is probably good enough, but I'll tell 'em once more."

I nodded, then clucked to the mule and kicked his sides. He stretched out at a fast walk when he realized we were heading home. It was after sundown when I got close enough to see our place. My hands ached from the cold and my toes felt as though they had frozen solid, but all I could think about was how happy I'd be to see the look on Ma's face when she pulled the bacon from the sack.

Closer to the cabin, the first thing I noticed was the door to the corncrib. It was open and a lantern burned inside. As I rode by, I saw Pa. He didn't seem to be doing anything other than standing to look at the meager contents. He glanced up but only shook his head before turning to concentrate on the ears of dried corn on the floor.

I rode on past the barn to the door of the dugout. "Ma?"

She opened the door in a rush. "Branson, where have you been? It's almost dark and I've been worried sick about you."

I felt an instant shame that I had deceived her, but it was

short-lived as I held the sack in her direction.

She stepped out of the dugout to take it. I anticipated her expression with great excitement, but I was surprised. She opened the sack, gasped and looked toward the barn and corncrib.

"Where did you get this?"

I pointed over my shoulder. "I worked today for Mr. and Mrs. Grunwald."

She glanced again to the barn. "Go put Jackson up, but don't say anything about this to your father." She turned abruptly and marched back through the door.

I was confused. She hadn't seemed as happy as I had expected. In fact, she seemed almost upset. I shook my head and turned the mule toward the barn. Once on the powdery dirt of the pen, he sniffed the ground then gingerly dropped to his knees, then to his hocks, and finally to his side to roll with four feet in the air. I watched for a moment before hanging the bridle on a post and hurrying to the house.

Ma sat at the table with Myrtle on her lap while Caleb held Josiah. A bowl of mush occupied the space in front of each and another waited for me on the rough plank table. I entered and pulled the door closed, then unbuttoned my coat and hung it on a peg.

"Hey, where'd you get that shirt?"

I turned to Caleb, anxious to tell him and Ma about my day, but I caught a subtle shaking of her head. The meaning was clear. Don't tell. I shrugged in hurried thought while stepping to my place at the table. "While I was out gathering wood I run across some folks in a wagon. They gave it to me." It was a pitiful excuse, but it was the best I could come up within the sudden moment. I'll admit that at the Grunwald's that day, I had fibbed a might about my age and my experience with an ax, but I'd been taught to tell the truth and the small lie tasted funny as it passed my lips, especially to my own family. I glanced at Ma. She nodded what I took for appreciation.

She cleared her throat. "Branson, would you please take the shirt off and leave it in your room?"

It was obvious she wanted to keep my visit to our neighbors a secret, but I couldn't figure out why. I'd done nothing wrong, I'd been paid for the work I did. I hadn't stolen the bacon or the shirt. I was confused, but I rose and did what I was told.

After tossing the flannel shirt to the corn shucks on the floor, I returned and sat at the table to look at the bowl of boiled grain. If it had been unappetizing at the start of the day, it was even more so after having been fed an unbelievable meal at lunch. I also knew there was bacon somewhere in the cabin. I stirred the mush and forced a spoonful into my mouth for no other reason than to keep Caleb from asking more questions. I continued until I couldn't stand another bite.

I glanced out the window and saw that darkness had come to the prairie. I stood. "Thanks for supper, Ma."

She scowled at me and it pained me to see her upset. I thought I'd done a good thing, but at the way she was acting, I wasn't so sure, although for the life of me I didn't know why.

Her face softened. "Thank you, Branson. "Will you help me get the kids to bed?"

"Yes, ma'am."

The door opened and Pa entered. He hung his worn felt hat on a peg then did the same with his too-thin coat. He turned and glared at me with hard eyes and gritted teeth. "Where have you been young man?"

I glanced quickly at Ma but she had her head down. I was on my own. I swallowed. "On the prairie. I've gathered a good stack of wood and can bring it back tomorrow." I looked away, hoping he believed my second lie of the night.

He grunted and it appeared as though he would leave it

lay, but of a sudden, he rose up and pointed a long finger. "It better be a stack and then some. We have chores to do here to get ready for planting in a few months and I won't have you wandering all over the country shirking your work here." He turned and stomped into the other room.

I looked at Ma. Her eyes were fearful and she held her bottom lip in her teeth. She mouthed the words, "We'll talk later." Without another word, she passed Myrtle to me.

I retook my seat on the bench and held my sister close, rocking back and forth while humming a tune. Her eyes grew heavy and in a few minutes she was asleep, as was Josiah in Ma's arms. Ma stepped into her room to put Josiah to bed then came back in a moment to take Myrtle from me.

When she returned, she touched Caleb on a shoulder. "Go on to bed, Son. Branson will help me with the dishes, then he'll be in to bed soon enough."

"Yes, ma'am." He removed Ma's sweater and passed it to her. She pushed her arms into the sleeves and pulled it close around her shoulders.

It was then that I realized that Ma had gone the entire day with only her thin dress for protection from the cold. With sudden guilt, I thought of the scant woodpile, and a quick glance to the floor next to the stove saw barely enough wood for the morning fire.

She turned her back to me to take a bucket from the stovetop and pour the water into the wash pan. She sighed as she began scrubbing the bowls and cookpot. I walked to her side and dried the dishes after she rinsed them in the bucket of clean water. It took only a few minutes to complete the task and she did not speak during that time. I hadn't either since I didn't know what to say. She stepped to the door and after two steps into the yard, flung the water from the dishpan to the packed dirt. She returned and closed the door, then motioned for me to join her in the bedroom where Caleb slept.

She leaned over him to make sure he was asleep. Satisfied, she sat on the floor and leaned against the dirt wall while patting a space next to her. "Sit here, Branson."

I slid to the ground and sat with my elbows on my knees. "Did I do wrong?"

She reached her arm over my shoulders and hugged me tightly. "No, Branson. What you did was honest and good. You saw an opportunity and you took it. I'm proud of you and even prouder because your first thought was to help our family."

I frowned. My ten-year-old brain tried to understand, but I couldn't figure it out. "Then why are you upset?"

She sighed as she leaned back. "I'm not upset at you, Branson." She regarded me and I saw the first makings of tears in her eyes.

"Then what's wrong?"

With a tilt of her head she looked through the opening toward her and Pa's room. She held her bottom lip in her teeth and gestured toward the other side of the cabin. "Your pa is feeling a might shaken right now."

"Shaken?"

"Yes, shaken. He feels like he's not enough."

Nothing was making sense. What did that mean? "Enough of what?"

She pulled me close and held my head to her breast, rubbing her fingers through my hair. I could feel the slow rise and fall of her chest as she breathed.

"Enough of a man, I suppose. He had such grand plans when we took over this homestead. But—."

"But what?"

She gently kissed the top of my head. "But he's tired and feels tied down."

I breathed in the smell of her and snuggled closer. "Is that why he goes to the marsh?"

Her fingers combed across my head as she took a deep

breath. "You know about his traps?"

I pulled away so I could see her face. "Yes. Caleb and I followed him once. There are no traps, are there?"

A sadness like I'd never seen came to her face. "No. Only a moment to himself so he can dream about the life he wishes he had."

I gazed toward the other room. "What does he wish for?"

Her frown deepened. "I don't think he knows for sure. One day he talks of owning a fine house surrounded by green fields and a new carriage pulled by a matched team of horses. Then the next day he wants action and adventure, to go places and do things." She tucked the wisps of hair behind her ears. "But the farm holds him fast with no escape."

I peered at her with wide-eyed innocence. "I don't understand. What does that have to do with me going to the Grunwald's to work? I had hoped that bringing the bacon would make you happy."

"I am happy." She paused. "But to him, you going to work for them to help support the family is a slap in his face. If he was a better provider, you wouldn't need to do that."

I rubbed my brow. For the first time I began in a small way to see the homestead through Pa's eyes. Four seasons every year of backbreaking work with high hopes, then the crickets or the hail would come, or too much rain or not enough. I thought of seeing him standing in the corncrib only an hour earlier. I began to understand that his hope for the future faded with each passing day.

I looked into her face. "But I don't mind helping. The Grunwalds said I could come once a week during the winter. I'll give my earnings to Pa so he can buy whatever he needs."

"I know, Son, and I love you for your willingness, but it would be a constant reminder to him that he wasn't good enough to make a living on his own."

I loved my Pa, but I realized with sudden clarity that his stubbornness was the cause for many of our problems. "Then we will eat mush and nothing more for the rest of the winter?"

She blinked hard, as though her eyes hurt. "I—."

I regretted the question, and even in my young age, I could see it pained her. "I'm sorry, Ma."

She pulled me close and kissed my forehead. "It's not your fault. Let's see what the morning brings." She released my face and smiled with her eyes dancing. "Now, tell me about your day at the Grunwald's."

I excitedly told her of meeting Curley, the peaches, the chicken and dumplings meal, and how I'd refused the fifty-cent payment for brushing only sixteen horses.

She nodded approvingly. "You did good. I'm sure they were impressed."

"They said I could come back once a week and work if it was all right with Pa."

Her eyes grew clouded again. "You let me work on that, but for the time being, don't wear the shirt until I figure out what to do."

I woke the next morning to the sound of Ma working at the stove. I pulled my overalls on quickly then slipped into my boots and strode into the kitchen.

Ma turned when she heard me and in her turning I could see the pan of boiling water for the mush. I frowned without thinking. I'd had my mind set on bacon, and seeing the mush bowl was a disappointment.

A small grimace appeared on her face. "Sorry, Son. Give me a day or two to decide how to tell your Pa."

I looked quickly to make sure he wasn't in the room.

She saw my glance. "He's outside. Said he was going to mend some harness this morning."

I nodded in relief. "I'm sorry I brought it home."

"Branson, never be sorry for doing a good thing. I'll figure it out, I only need a little time."

"Yes, ma'am." I reached for my coat and with a deep

breath, opened the door and stepped into the frigid wind.

Three armloads of wood later, I sat for a quick bowl of mush. I forced myself to eat enough to give me some strength for the day, then I stood. "I'll catch Jackson and scamper to find some wood. I'll be back before noon."

"Thank you, Son." She reached and caressed my back. "Go put that flannel shirt on. I will help keep a little warmth in today."

"Thanks, Ma."

Jackson stood at the far side of the corral as I approached. He ate from a sparse pile of prairie hay that Pa had thrown in. I took the bridle from the post and gently slipped the bit into his mouth, then led him to the barn. Pa sat on a stool next to a wall with harness straps over his knees and a needle and spool of thick thread.

"Morning, Pa."

He stopped his sewing only long enough to glance up. "Morning." He motioned toward the mule. "Going out to get that pile of wood?" He dropped his head to push the needle through a stitching hole in the harness.

"Yes, sir." I reached above his shoulder to retrieve Jackson's collar with brass knobs which I carried outside and slipped over the mule's head, then after another trip inside for a thirty-foot coil of rope that I hung over one of the knobs, I leaned in. "I'll be back before noon."

He grunted without looking up.

I rode west, toward the Grunwald's because I'd seen two downed trees on the path. They were small enough for Jackson to drag back and big enough to supply the much-needed wood.

The overhead sun warmed my back and to my relief, the wind was barely more than a breeze. If I hadn't known better, I'd have sworn that a glimpse of spring was in the air. The downed trees lay within thirty yards of each other. I ran the loop of the rope around one to drag it to the other, then with a loop around both and the end tied to the mule's collar, I headed home. When I topped the rise and looked down on our little piece of the prairie, I thought I caught the faintest sniff of cooking bacon. I gazed at the smoke coming from the chimney and hurried my pace. The closer I got, the more I knew that the smell was real and I wasn't dreaming. I dragged the trees as close as I could, then untied the rope from Jackson's collar. Letting him stand to graze on the sparse grass and weeds around the dugout, I hurried to the door and stepped inside.

Caleb stood over the pan intently watching the sizzling bacon. His wide eyes and unrestrained smile told the story I wanted to hear. The aroma was overpowering. I stopped and closed my eyes and breathed deeply, filling my nostrils with the heavenly smell. I opened my eyes, anxious to see the look on Ma's face, but she didn't look as happy as I thought she should.

She raised her eyebrows. "Right on time. Grab Myrtle from the floor and take a seat."

I grabbed my sister, lifting and tickling her to get a laugh. She obliged and I joined in the glee. After sitting on the bench, I looked at Ma. "Where's Pa?" I had hoped he would also be enjoying the smell and anticipation, and I likewise hoped he would smile at me, maybe even tell me I'd done good.

The corners of her mouth turned downward. "He went to check his traps."

My lips pressed together of their own accord. "Because of the bacon?"

"Yes, but don't you worry about that. Let's eat and enjoy."

Randall Dale

Chapter 4

We surrounded the table, Caleb next to Ma who held Josiah, and me on the other side holding Myrtle. For the longest time, those of us old enough to know, stared at the plate of bacon. Finally, Caleb turned to Ma. She gave him a nod of permission so he reached and carefully pinched a piece and held it to his nose. After a long, deep breath, he took a small bite. He closed his eyes and chewed slowly, savoring the meat with an ecstasy seldom enjoyed in our little cabin.

Ma leaned forward to push a piece of bacon to Myrtle then pulled one close for Josiah. Neither of the toddlers showed the restraint Caleb had shown. They both chomped greedily and the small strips disappeared almost instantly. I waited for Ma, for I wanted to see the look on her face when she tasted the meat, but she sat unmoving with arms around Josiah. She lay her chin on his blond head and watched with no joy.

I loved her so and I hated seeing her unhappy.

She smiled bravely. "Go on, Branson. You get one piece

too."

A single strip of the meat remained on the plate and I realized that if I took it, she would get none. I wanted the bacon, wanted it with my whole soul, but my arm would not reach to the center of the table. I slowly shook my head. "I want you to have it."

A wail emerged from deep in her chest and she buried her head in Josiah's collar. Her shoulders shook as she sobbed. I wanted to comfort her, but what could I do?

Finally, she took a deep breath and raised her head. "How about we share?"

I smiled my acceptance of her offer. "I'd like that."

She leaned again and held the meat in two hands. I shook my head when I saw she held it so at the breaking, one piece would be larger. She smiled as she passed it to me and plopped the smaller piece into her mouth.

I took my morsel, studied it carefully and smelled it one more time, then, as Caleb had done, took small bites and chewed slowly, feeling every sensation and filling my head with the taste of the salt, smoke and meat flavor.

When the fragment was gone I sat with my eyes closed remembering the exquisite flavor. The door suddenly crashed open and my eyes flew there to see the silhouette of Pa standing in the entrance. His face showed deep lines and his eyes bored into me as he pointed.

His boots drug across the swept, dirt floor. "You are never to go to the Grunwald's again, you understand me?"

I had never seen him so angry. I shrank back, afraid for my safety. He'd never hit me, other than an occasional swat across my behind if I'd misbehaved, but this time was different. His rage was beyond anything I'd seen. My chest felt cold and empty as I stared at him in fear.

Ma reached to touch his arm but he jerked away and shot a glance of warning at her. I stepped forward quickly, afraid of what he might do to me, but more afraid of what he might do to her.

"Yes, sir. I'll never go again."

He turned to me and I saw the anger that burned in his eyes slowly diminish until they seemed almost lifeless. His shoulders sagged as he stepped back and turned out the door.

The twins cried loudly and Caleb and I stared, wide-eyed, at Ma. She pressed Josiah to her chest and wiped a tear from her cheek with the shoulder of her dress. I passed Myrtle to Caleb and stepped to Ma's side, pressing my cheek against hers.

"I'm sorry, Ma. I wish I'd never gone over there."

With one arm she hugged me then moved her head to kiss my cheek. "What you did was good, Branson. Your Pa isn't as much upset with you as he is with himself. Do you remember what I said last night, that he would think the bacon you brought was a glaring reminder that he was letting us down by not providing adequately for us?"

I remembered what she had said and I had thought about it aplenty in the night, but no matter how much I thought about it, I could not understand. If he wanted more for us, then why wouldn't he let me help?

"Why, Ma?"

She shook her head and held Josiah to her shoulder and stroked his hair. She gazed at me with a lonely expression. "Maybe you'll understand when you get older." She gently touched my arm. "We'll make do. This year will be a good crop and everyone will get a new coat and boots."

The days ran on and months passed. I turned eleven before the last frost and spring planting was upon us. The bacon lasted for the rest of the winter because Ma only cooked enough for us to get a tiny taste. But it was a welcome taste, although I don't recall Pa ever eating a single piece. He never said another word about the Grunwalds, and with spring plowing and planting, I didn't have a chance to go anyway.

That year's crop was much better'n we'd had for some time, maybe even the best we'd ever had. It was late fall, after the crop was sold, that Pa loaded us into our rickety wagon and bundled us against the cold with blankets from the house. Ma was in a festive mood, sitting close to Pa and hugging his arm while holding a worn, patchwork quilt over her shoulders. Old Jackson leaned into his collar when Pa called for him to giddup, and the wagon creaked into motion. Our only stop was the mercantile store. Pa lifted Ma from the wagon and placed her gently on the dirt of the street. His expression showed a gaiety I'd never seen. As a family, we stepped into the store.

Pa hollered to Mr. Smithson, the owner. "Peter, a hard piece of candy for each of the young'uns."

I looked at Ma. She smiled and nodded. I could hardly believe it. I hadn't had a piece of hard candy since the Parson Whitaker came calling when I was along about six or so. The candy was the only thing about his visit I could remember, but I do recall always wishing he would come back and bring some more. Although Ma used the bible to teach us to read, we weren't church-goers, so I suppose he never saw any reason for another visit.

Mr. Smithson smiled, wedged his ample frame behind the counter and lifted the lid from the glass jar. When he reached in, he pulled out four candies and passed them to me. I gave one each to Caleb and the twins then plopped the other into my mouth.

Ma stepped to the owner with a list, which she passed over. His eyes grew wide and he looked up with a frown.

He looked from Ma to Pa. "Henry, I can't give you credit for this much."

Pa reached into his pocket and pulled something and slapped it on the counter next to the candy jars. When he pulled his hand away, a twenty-dollar gold piece, shining in the light coming in through the front windows, remained. "I reckon this ought to cover it and then some."

I had never seen a twenty-dollar gold piece, and from the expression on the store owner's face, I wondered if he'd seen all that many himself. And I know he'd never seen one from Pa.

Smithson grinned. "Yes, sir." He then bustled through the store, bringing food and supplies to the counter, and none of the supplies were as welcome a sight as a cloth-covered side of bacon.

The twins, Caleb and I sat on a hard bench next to a checkerboard. An oversized, pot-bellied stove put out just enough heat to keep the store comfortable. I got to watching Pa. He stood in the middle of the store, one arm folded and his chin resting on the knuckles of his free hand. His gaze seemed fixed on the wall above the storekeepers head. I turned to look and saw what held Pa's attention. It was a rifle with a polished wood stock and long barrel. It looked to be as long as I was tall.

He looked down at me, then motioned to the rifle with his nose. "I'm needing a new rifle since that old flintlock split its barrel. If we had a rifle, we could hunt for our winter meat again."

I nodded. Many was the time while out gathering wood I'd seen deer, or rabbits, and once, a small herd of buffalo. He was right. With a gun, we wouldn't need to have mush three times a day for weeks on end, and with any luck, he might even let me learn to shoot.

He put a hand on my shoulder. "Recon you could handle a gun?"

I looked into Pa's face. I'd never seen him act that way. He actually smiled at me. I could not recall him ever smiling at me like that before.

I looked up in hopefulness, unsure if I had heard correctly. "Yes, sir."

He squeezed my neck gently, then pulled me along as he stepped to the counter.

Smithson looked up. "Yes, Henry?"

Pa pushed his floppy hat back on his head then motioned to the wall. "Let us take a look at your rifle?"

Smithson turned and looked up, then stood on tiptoes, hefted the rifle down and passed it to Pa. "It's a somewhat new design with a percussion cap instead of the old flintlock." He reached under the counter and brought out a small box. After opening it, he slid a tiny cylinder across the counter. "It's much more reliable and you won't get the misfires that were so common with the old style."

I had no idea what the man was talking about, but I supposed Pa did. He brought the rifle to his shoulder and held it in firing position, sighting down the barrel at a shelf of blankets on the back wall.

Pa placed the rifle back to the counter and picked up the percussion cap. He studied it for a moment then slid it back. He stood to full height. "How much?"

Smithson replaced the cap to the box, closed the lid and bent to return it to its rightful place under the counter. When he stood, he looked at Pa while squinting one eye. "Rifle, a supply of balls, powder and percussion caps," he paused and tilted his head. "seventeen dollars."

My hopes had been high, but the mention of the price sucked the air out of me like I'd stepped from a warm cabin into a bitter, winter wind. To my knowledge, we'd never had more'n twenty dollars the whole time we'd been on the homestead, and the food and supplies stacked in front of Mr. Smithson would certainly take most of the gold piece Pa had slapped on the counter. I looked at the wooden floor and felt bad for Pa. It was plain to see he wanted the rifle, and wanted it some powerful. I wanted it too, not only for the meat it would bring to our table, but to have a chance to learn to shoot. As I stared at the floor, I waited for Pa to step back or to let out a low whistle and shake his head, but there was only silence.

I chanced a glance to Pa, fully expecting to see an expression of shock at the high price, but I was surprised. Instead of slouching in dismay, he stood straight with shoulders back and thumbs tucked into the front of his pants. He looked at me with a tiny grin, then he winked.

I'd never seen Pa wink and could have probably counted on one hand the number of times I'd seen him smile, but there he was, looking at me with a twinkle in his eye.

He turned to Mr. Smithson, then plunged his hand deep into his pocket and pulled out another coin, which he flipped to the counter. It bounced and rolled and would have fallen to the floor had Mr. Smithson not slapped it with his palm. The storekeeper slowly lifted his hand. I stepped forward to see a gleaming, double eagle identical to the one Pa had passed over only ten minutes earlier. I swallowed hard and felt like my eyes would fall out of my head.

Smithson picked the coin from the counter and turned it front to back and back to front. He rubbed his fingers over the engraving and acted as surprised as I was. I'm sure he, like me, had never seen Pa with that much money. He flipped the coin in the air and caught it on the way down, then smiled with a nod. After slipping the piece into his pocket, he lifted the rifle and passed it over.

The drive home was pleasant. Caleb and I held the twins in the back of the wagon while Ma held Pa's arm tightly and leaned her head on his shoulder as they sat on the seat. I couldn't take my eyes from the long rifle resting against the side of the wagon. I couldn't see the rifle, of course, because it was wrapped in a blanket to keep it from damage, but I knew it was there and my imaginations ran wild with thoughts of shooting game on the Kansas prairie.

We ate supper in the dugout that night, then Pa sat at the table and unwrapped the rifle and held it between his legs with the butt on the floor and barrel pointing to the roof. Ma worked to get the twins in bed, but Caleb and I sat on the dirt floor and listened and watched as Pa taught us about guns. He showed us how to measure the powder and how to tamp the ball into the barrel. He showed us where the percussion cap went and how it worked, although he never actually put one under the hammer for fear of accidental firing. I went to bed that night with dreams of standing in a meadow with the long barrel stretched out pointed at a deer.

That winter was the best I could remember. Each of us had a new coat and Caleb and I had new boots. We had meat on the table and only ate mush on occasion, and always with molasses. Pa took the rifle out regular and more often than not he came back successful. If my chores were done, he let me go with him and he taught me how to charge, load and tamp the ball home, but he didn't allow me to shoot because powder and balls were too expensive. I didn't care, it was enough to be with Pa. He seemed genuinely happy, and he came in at the end of each day with a smile on his face and a hug for Ma. As I thought about those glorious short months, I realized his trips to check his traps became less frequent.

With the coming of the spring of 1861, the rifle was placed on two pegs over the door and farm work began again. Old Jackson, stronger with winter rest and ample feed, leaned into his collar when I clucked to him. I had turned twelve, and with a better diet, had grown. Pa took the plow and we watched with pleasure as it sliced through the moist earth. Caleb and I walked behind, using a pointed stick to make holes and dropping one seed in each, then stepping on the hole so the corn would sprout. For the first time in my memory, it looked like we would get the planting finished on time. It seemed that luck was finally starting to shine on the Hawk family in Lawrence, Kansas, and Pa's cheer lifted the whole family.

Within three weeks the corn shoots were six inches tall and it seemed we might have two years in a row of good harvest, but old Mother Nature had different plans. No rain in May caused the earth to dry and the plants to stunt. Hot, dry weeks went by and the sunburned leaves of the knee-high corn plants stood motionless in the relentless June heat. The hope we'd felt at the ideal conditions of spring faded as we watched the withering plants in the field. The smiles that had been so common only a month prior were replaced with grim faces and solemn glances. Every day the beating sun in the cloudless sky pulled all the moisture from the plants, and all hope from us. Ma prayed each night for rain, but at our waking in the morning, we could do no more than prepare ourselves for another dry day in the scorching sun. Pa's gaiety that we had enjoyed during the winter was forgotten. He became morose and uncommunicative and spent more time checking his traps. Ma tried to reassure him, but the old Pa, the familiar Pa, had returned.

We sat around the table finishing the last of a meager meal in the sweltering heat of sundown in late July. No one spoke. Even the twins sensed the gloominess and made no sound. I jumped when a call came from outside.

"Hello the house."

Pa frowned as he looked up. He glanced at Ma, then stood and pulled the rope handle of the door and stepped outside. I watched Ma. She shrugged as she got up to clear the table. I let Josiah slide to the floor then I joined her and pulled a dishtowel from a nail on the wall. She washed and I dried, all the while wondering who had come calling.

Boots scraped against the cut steps so I looked to the door. "Bull Jameson, one of Pa's friends from town, ducked to enter the dugout holding his hat in his hands.

He nodded to Ma. "Mrs. Hawk."

She wiped her hands on her apron. "Hello, Bull."

Pa entered to stand next to our visitor. He looked directly

at Ma. "Bull says the slave states have left from the Union and there is a war."

Ma blinked. "What?"

Bull slapped his hat on his thigh. "That's right ma'am. I can't believe you haven't heard. It's been going on for near three months now."

Ma turned to see Pa, then looked at Bull again. "We haven't been to town since the fall."

He shrugged. "Well, there's a ruckus going on and their calling for men to go fight. I'm leaving for Leavenworth in the morning to join up. I just wanted to stop by and say my goodbyes." He stepped back and mashed his hat on his head while eyeing Pa. "You decide quick, now, hear?" He climbed the steps and disappeared in the increasing darkness.

Ma stepped toward Pa. "Decide about what?"

He studied the ground and didn't answer for a time.

She stepped closer. "Henry?"

His lips pursed tightly and I could see his jaw muscles under his skin. He swallowed then looked to her. "I'm going too."

She jerked her head. "Going where?"

"To Leavenworth to join up." His eyes were pleading as he gazed at her.

"Why on earth would you do that?"

He turned his head to see me, then Caleb and finally the twins. His shoulders looked like he had the weight of a millstone on his neck. He took a deep breath. "Katherine, I'm no farmer." He waved his arm in a wide arc. "We have no crop this year, no money to buy food or clothes and no hope that things will get better." He motioned with his head to the door. "Bull says they will pay. I'll send you money every month. I don't know what else I can do."

Tears sprang to her eyes. "We can make do. We always come out all right in the end. Next year will be better."

He shook his head. "Bull says the war won't last but

another few months. If I don't go now it will be too late. I'll go and fight and send the money every month. My mind is made up. I'll leave in the morning and be home before it gets cold. I promise."

She made no answer and it surprised me. I was mostly certain her thoughts were the same as mine. How could he leave? How could he abandon us? My thoughts turned to her and what she must be feeling. Why didn't she ask? I studied the side of her face. Her bottom lip curled outward in a pout and her chin quivered as she held his gaze. He leaned forward, his face sad and somber in the light of the coal oil lantern. The moment passed and I watched her expression stiffen. She blinked away the tears, took a deep breath and stood taller. She gave Pa a slow nod, then, without a word, she turned back to the dishpan.

Pa waited for a moment, I suppose in hopes she would turn to him again, to talk to him, but she made no movement other than the slow and steady rubbing of the dishes in the pan. His shoulders sagged as he turned to step out the door.

His call was loud. "Bull! Stop by here in the morning and I'll go with you."

As Ma heard it she let out a small gasp followed by a sob, but by the time Pa returned to the dugout, she had swallowed the pain and fear and acted as though nothing was wrong. But I knew the life as we knew it was about to change.

Randall Dale

Chapter 5

The first rays of the rising sun cast long shadows at the front of our little dugout as we lined up. Bull leaned on the corral post, far enough away to give us some privacy for our goodbyes. Josiah and Myrtle held to Ma's legs while Caleb and I stood on either side. Pa placed his little bundle on the ground and grabbed both of my shoulders in his big hands.

"Use the rifle and keep the family fed until I get home."

"Yes, sir." I wanted to say more, to ask him why he was leaving us, but I held my tongue. I swallowed and viewed the dust between my boots because I didn't want him to see the tears in my eyes. He cupped the back of my neck and pulled me to his cheek where I was surprised to feel the wetness of his tear. If nothing else, it made me feel better to know his leaving was hard on him too.

He did the same to Caleb, then knelt and hugged the twins. He grunted as he pushed to his feet. He looked at Ma and swallowed hard, then held her face in both hands to hold his forehead to hers. They stood there for a long time, eyes closed, unmoving. Tears ran from each of their faces and dripped from their cheeks.

Bull cleared his throat. "Henry, we'd best be leaving."

Pa sighed and stepped back. "I love you all." He said it quickly, then stared for a long moment. With a shake of his head, he turned to Bull. "Let's go then."

Ma tousled Josiah's hair with one hand and waved her white handkerchief with the other, continuing until Pa was out of sight. Only then did a wail escape her chest. In instant weakness, she fell to her knees with her fists to her eyes.

I didn't know what to do. I touched her shoulder. "Ma?"

She looked up and wiped her tears with the backs of her hands. Her eyes roamed from each of the twins, to Caleb, and finally to me. With pursed lips, she bravely nodded and pushed to her feet. She gazed one last time to the path, but Pa was gone. She smiled weakly. "Come inside." She spread her arms and herded us through the door like a mother hen with baby chicks.

She pointed to the table. "Caleb, Branson, sit."

We sat while the twins wandered about the small room finding ways to make a mess. Ma ignored them while looking intensely at Caleb, then at me.

"Branson, you are the man of the house now. It will be up to you to keep us fed."

I nodded. "Yes, ma'am. I can do that."

She turned to Caleb. "Caleb, most of Branson's chores will fall to you. Can you keep the woodpile stacked and full and Old Jackson fed every day?"

"Yes, ma'am."

"Good." She tilted her head. "It will be like a game to see how we do while your Pa's away."

I smiled, even though it was the last thing I wanted to do. I decided I would be brave for Ma because I could see she was trying to be brave for us.

I stood and reached for my summer hat, a floppy, hand-me-down felt that would keep my ears from getting burned by the unforgiving sun. I pulled it to my head. "I'll catch Jackson and slip on down to the breaks to see what I can find." I pulled a chair to reach the rifle over the door, then walked out with the long rifle in two hands.

Sweat rolled down my back as the morning sun beat on my shoulders. I rode west and some south, toward the uneven prairie not too far from the Grunwald's place where I could stalk any animals I might find. I held the long rifle balanced over Jackson's withers and pushed him forward with constant kicking. In the distance, I saw an old gnarled, windblown tree and planned on a short rest there in the inviting shade. As I approached, a pheasant ran, then flew to a bush fifty yards away. I pulled Old Jackson to a stop, slid from his back and stepped in front to take a knee. From a small bag tied around my neck, I took a percussion cap and placed it under the hammer. I sat on my foot and rested my arm on a knee in a firing position. The bird looked nervous and ready for flight so I jerked the trigger to shoot before he escaped. The gun roared but the pheasant lifted and flew unharmed far into the prairie.

I gritted my teeth in disgust for I'd wanted to take a meal home for Ma, but the bird was gone and I was a cap and ball lighter. I loaded, measuring and pouring the powder and carefully placing the patch over the bore and the ball over the patch. With my thumb I pushed it down into the barrel and lightly drove everything home with the tamping rod. If I saw another animal, I'd only have to set the cap and be ready to shoot.

The sun-scorched land offered no additional prospect of shade as I rode toward the breaks. Old Jackson dropped his head and shambled along in weary steadiness and I found my own eyelids growing heavy. My head jerked as Jackson stopped suddenly and studied the trail to our front. His ears pointed forward and I squinted to search for what he might have seen.

When I realized a big, partially concealed buck stood staring back at me from only thirty yards away, my heart raced. I dared not move, for I knew he'd be gone at the first sign of danger. The deer lifted his nose and sniffed the air. When he cocked his head, the sun glinted off his antlers.

After staring at us for a full minute, he used his antlers to scratch his back, then took several steps before lowering his head to graze on the prairie grass and brush. I slipped as quietly as I could to the ground and took three measured steps away from my mule, then squatted to the ground as I'd done while attempting to shoot the pheasant. I placed the cap, then pulled the hammer back with a loud click. I cringed, hoping that the sound had not scared the deer.

I raised my head above the grass expecting to see the buck, but had no luck because he stood in a depression out of my sight. I stood slowly and peered to where I'd seen him last, happy to see the buck continuing to graze, unconcerned that Jackson and I had invaded his territory. Slowly, so as not to scare the animal, I raised the rifle and sighted down the barrel. I took a deep breath and jerked the trigger.

I knew as soon as the shot was away that I'd missed. The buck jumped high enough to have cleared our barn, then he fled, bounding through the breaks and disappearing into the distance. I stomped my foot. I'd wasted two charges of powder and two balls that day. If I didn't start aiming better, our meager shooting supplies would be gone much too fast.

Jackson stood without protest as I jumped and shimmied onto his back. I glanced toward the sun, noticing it had already passed the midway point of the day. I looked forward, trying to decide if I should continue or turn for home. I was so intent on the view of the breaks that I didn't hear the footfalls of a horse coming from behind.

"Hello."

Jackson must not have heard either, because he jumped, and between his jumping and my jerking around to see where the voice had come from, I fell to the ground, landing flat on my back while holding the rifle to my chest. I couldn't breathe and I thought I would die before I could get any air into my lungs.

Someone stepped to my side but I didn't know who it was because the unblocked, overhead sun in my eyes blinded me, and I was so worried about getting my breath, I didn't much care who the man was anyway.

After what seemed an eternity, I took a breath and rolled to my side. The man knelt and held his hand over my brow to block the sun."

"Well glory be, if it ain't Mr. Hawk."

I rolled to my knees and rested there gasping. I looked up, squinting, and recognized the pleasant black face and white hair of Curley from the Grunwald's place. I had wondered if he was still around. I hadn't seen him since my only visit a year and a half earlier, but I had enjoyed sharing the peaches with him and I still remembered fondly his telling me I did good work.

"Hello, Mr. Curley." One of my hands held the rifle and the other held my belly.

He reached to grasp my wrist and pull me to my feet. "Not Mr. Curley, jus' Curley." He smiled as he lightly squeezed my shoulder. "What you be doing out here all by your lonesome?"

I tried for a deep breath, then placed the butt of the rifle on the ground. "Hunting."

He nodded knowingly. "I heard the shot. Let's go find your game and I'll help you with it."

A frown involuntarily came to my face. "I missed."

He joined me in my frowning. "Missed?"

My embarrassment was complete. Curley looked at me as though he couldn't believe I'd sent the ball anywhere but where I'd wanted it. I dropped my head. "Yes, sir."

He touched my shoulder again. "Don't you be fretting

about missing a shot. Heaven knows I missed many a shot when I was learning."

I grunted while shaking my head. It hadn't crossed my mind that Curley had learned to shoot. I had assumed his chores were limited to splitting wood or taking care of the horses as he had done when I was there so many months before. And besides, why would a rich man's hired hand need to know how to shoot?

He chuckled good-naturedly as he read my face. "So, you don't think I knows how to shoot that there rifle?" He motioned toward the gun I held in my hands. He held his oversized hands out. "Let me see that there thing."

My knuckles turned white as I gripped all the tighter. I don't know why I did it. It wasn't that I didn't trust him, or that I was afraid that he'd steal it. I suppose it was that I'd been trusted with it by my Pa and that meant keeping it in my possession at all times.

He grinned as he folded his arms over his massive chest. "That be all right. Good for you to be keeping it close, and shame on me for asking. I'll not ask you for it again."

Relief filled my chest, but embarrassment that I'd treated him ill soon rooted it out and took its place. "I'm sorry. It's Pa's gun and he trusted me with it." I felt so bad that I pushed the rifle toward him, but his arms remained folded and he wouldn't take it from me.

"You did right." He cocked his head. "Where your pa be?"

Jackson stomped at a fly and I turned to look at him, thankful that Curley couldn't see my face. I didn't want to answer his question because I was ashamed that Pa had lit out and left us to fend for ourselves. The silence in the air was loud in my ears. Deep down I wanted someone to confide in, someone to tell my feelings to. I couldn't tell Ma because she counted on me and I didn't want her to worry any more than she already was. But Curley was almost a stranger and he wouldn't understand anyway.

He stared, content to wait without speaking.

It was the silence, I suppose, that broke me down. My bottom lip curled downward and my chin dropped to my chest as I choked back the sobs. He reached to pull me close, holding me in a gentle embrace for a long minute. At any other time it would have seemed odd. He didn't know me and I didn't know him. He was a man and I was a boy and he had no reason to hold me in the tender hug, but I was glad he did, for no matter how much I thought otherwise, I needed comfort.

He stroked my hair as I cried into his chest. "You's a good boy, young Branson Hawk. I knew that the first day you come for a visit." He held me tight and patted my back. When my sobs finally subsided, he pushed me back and leaned to look into my tear-filled eyes. "There be times when a man needs to have a good cry. Lord knows I've had my share. I don't know why you be feeling like you do and you don't need to tell me, but if you ever need someone to sit and listen, I be here."

I took half a step back and wiped my eyes and face with my fingers. As I looked at Curley, I was certain his eyes were also moist.

When the words came I couldn't stop them. "My Pa's done left to fight in the war. We are all alone with no money and no crop. I'm supposed to keep meat on the table, but I can't hit anything I shoot at." I held the rifle up for him to see. "Ma, Caleb and the twins are counting on me, and I'm scared."

He took a deep breath and somehow in his dark eyes, I hoped I could see that he understood. I wiped my eyes again. "What if I can't keep meat on the table? What if I let them down?"

He took a moment to bend his hat brim up and look at the overhead sun with squinted eyes. When he turned back to me, he motioned toward my mule. "Step on your critter and I'll get on mine. There be a shade tree a half mile back." He walked with me to where Jackson grazed on the prairie grass, then bent and grabbed my hat from the ground. He placed it on my head and helped me onto Jackson's back. I balanced the rifle on the mule's withers and waited for Curley to mount his horse. We rode without speaking to the tree I'd been anxious to rest under only an hour earlier.

Curley dismounted, tied the reins around the horse's neck to allow him to graze, and motioned for me to do the same. I leaned the rifle against the tree, then we sat on a fallen log under the welcome shade.

The big man pushed his hat back on his head and wiped the sweat with his sleeve. He looked at me without speaking. It seemed he was trying to decide what to say. He plucked a grass stem and picked at his teeth for a moment, then folded his arms and leaned back. "I knows what it be like to be scared and alone."

I waited, anxious to hear how a big, strong man like him could be scared. I was sure he didn't know what it was like to be without a father. He could talk all he wanted, but he'd never been in my situation, he couldn't know what I felt.

A faraway look came into his eyes. He wouldn't look at me, but stared into the distance. It seemed a long time before he spoke again.

"I was eight-years-old." He stopped, his face showing remembered pain.

I leaned forward, drawn to the man and curious about the story he seemed ready to tell. Perhaps I'd been wrong. Perhaps he knew more about being alone than I'd thought. Curley continued to watch the horizon, but I knew he was seeing something from his past and not the cloudless blue of the summer Kansas sky.

He took a breath and started again. "I was eight-years-old. We had picked cotton all day for the master."

I blinked. He had been a slave!

"Afore I knowed what happened I was trussed up like a pig going to slaughter and throwed into a wagon. You can believe me when I tells you I know what it's like to be alone."

I swallowed and looked at him with wonder. "They took you away from your folks?"

"More'n a hundred miles. I never saw 'em again."

My eyes opened wide. I'd heard Ma and Pa talk about slavery and how evil it was, but until that moment, I had not understood. "Did you try to get away, to go back?"

He nodded sadly, then stood and turned his back to me. He reached and pulled his shirt to his neck as he bent over. I gasped at the deeply embedded, leather-like scars that covered his back.

He stood, pulled his shirt down and turned to me. I instinctively ran to him and hugged his neck. I had tried to be a man like Ma and Pa wanted, but in that instant, I was only a scared twelve-year-old boy trying to make sense of what was happening to me, and of what had happened to him. I wept into his neck, for I couldn't keep the sobs inside. Sobs of sadness for him, and for me.

In looking back, I suppose we were lucky that no one saw us. Folks around Lawrence, Kansas were mostly against slavery, but they still likely would not have approved of a white boy hugging a black man. But I hadn't yet learned the boundaries and I'm grateful that Curley could see how much I needed him at that moment.

He held me close with his muscular arms and for the first time since that morning, I felt safe.

He patted my back. "There, there. Everything gonna be all right."

I squeezed my eyes tight, trying to hold the tears in. When I released my grip, I stepped back to look into is broad face. "What should I do?"

He sat on the log and patted the space next to him in invitation for me to do the same. He rubbed his palms on his pants then looked at his hands and took a deep breath. At length he turned to me. "First thing you have to know is that you can't be changin' what's already done. All you can do is work to make things better from here on out."

"How can things be better? We have no crop, no money and no hope."

He shook his head. "There's always hope. It may not seem like it now, but you can't be givin' up." He stood and looked down at me with his dark eyes. "You a good boy, Branson, and you'll make a good man."

My shoulders slumped as I felt the responsibility of caring for our family, of being the man of the house, as Pa had called me. He'd told me to keep meat on the table, but how could I do that if I couldn't hit what I aimed at? I frowned at the times I had begged Pa to let me shoot, but he had refused with the excuse that we didn't have powder or balls to waste.

I gritted my teeth at the remembrance. He should have taught me. He should have been a better father. My emotions raced. I was suddenly furious at his leaving. He'd abandoned us, left us with nothing but worry and fear.

The thoughts tore at my insides, and my breath came in short, jerking gasps. My hands balled into fists and I hit the log on which I sat. "I hate him. I hope he never comes back." Then more quietly while holding my face in my hands, I repeated the words, "I hope he never comes back."

Big hands lifted me and held me close. "Get it on out, Branson. There be no shame in the way you be feeling. This is your time. You take it. When you be done, then it will be time to take care of your family."

I cried on his shoulder for a long minute, then stood and took a deep breath, embarrassed that I'd cried more in the last few minutes than I had in my entire life. I pointed to the rifle. "How can I take care of my family? Pa never taught me to shoot."

He paused for a moment with his thumbs tucked into the front of his pants. He cocked his head while looking at me, then walked to the trunk of the tree where Pa's rifle leaned. He turned back to me, waiting for permission to pick it up. When I realized what he wanted, I nodded. He smiled and reached for the gun, then studied it, turning it over in his meaty hands.

"A fine rifle."

I nodded again, but no matter how fine a rifle it was, it made no difference if I couldn't send the ball where I wanted it to go. "Yes, it is. I only wish I could use it like it was meant to be used."

He turned from me and raised the rifle to a shooting position, pointing it to the prairie. When he lowered it, he rubbed the stock and fingered the filigree of the action. He looked at me, then motioned with his head over his shoulder toward the Grunwald's place. "Mr. Grunwald, he taught me to shoot. How 'bout I teach you?"

I raised my head in hope, then just as quickly, dropped it again. "I don't have any powder or balls to spare. I can't waste any because I need to save all I have to hunt for meat."

He pursed his lips and nodded. "That be a wise thing to save your supplies. A man should always be thinking about the future." He studied the rifle again before glancing up. "But when it comes to shooting, and some other things I reckon, sometimes you have to use what you got early, so as to save what you got for later."

I frowned, not understanding.

He watched, then smiled. "Did you shoot at anything today?"

"Yes, sir. A pheasant and a buck."

"Missed both?"

I hung my head. "Yes, sir."

"And tomorrow, when you be finding some game and get a shot, will you be taking meat home to your family?"

I puffed my chest in false bluster. "Yes."

He didn't speak, he simply looked at me with his head tilted.

The longer he stood in silence, the more I knew that my answer had been foolish, and I was aware the he also knew. I dropped my head. "Probably not."

He smiled kindly and in it, I felt an inexplicable closeness with this man. I was scared, as he had once been scared, and as I remembered his story, I realized that he, at an even younger age, had been more alone than I was at that moment. Curley had treated me right at our first meeting at the Grunwald's place those many months earlier, and had continued in his caring this day. He had held me as I cried, had encouraged me in my hopelessness and had offered assistance in a time of helplessness. I realized I trusted him, and at that moment, I desperately needed someone to trust.

"What can I do?"

He passed the rifle to me. "Show me what you did when you shot at the pheasant."

My brow wrinkled in question, but I quickly decided that if I was to trust him, I would do so completely. I sat on my foot with the other knee raised and balanced the rifle in replication of the position I'd taken earlier.

He waited with arms folded. "I see. And the buck?"

I stood and pointed the rifle forward. As it grew heavy in my thin arms, I lowered it and turned to Curley.

He motioned to the rifle with his nose. "Heavy, ain't it?"

I lowered the rifle to the ground and held the barrel in my hand. It was almost as tall as I was. "Yes, sir."

He grinned and stepped closer. "When you are holding it, is the barrel steady on what you be aiming at?"

I grimaced. It was far from steady. It felt like I was standing on a moving wagon on a rock-filled road. I hung my head. "No, sir."

"Thought so." He grabbed my arm and guided me to the

log we'd used for sitting. "Kneel down behind the log and put the rifle on top."

I did as I was told, resting the long barrel on the log and pulling the stock close to my shoulder.

He pushed me forward with a gentle nudge. "Move on closer. Be putting your forearm on the log and the rifle in your hand."

I looked down the sights in awe and smiled as the front sight remained steady. I looked up into his face and saw an expression of glee.

"Makes a big difference don't it?"

My smile widened. "Yes, sir."

"That be your first lesson. Whene'er you can, you best find something solid for a brace." He tucked his thumbs into his armpits. "When you be older and stronger, you'll be able to hold it, but not yet." He looked into the prairie, then pointed to a bush. "I'll be right back."

He jogged to the bush and placed his hat on a waist-high branch, then hurried back. He grinned as he stepped over the log. "Load a ball."

I measured the powder and poured it into the barrel, then the patch and finally, the ball, tamping it home with the rod.

He watched with a nod. "Looks like you learned good. Now the cap."

After sliding the ramrod into its place under the barrel, I reached into the bag around my neck for a percussion cap. I extracted one and placed it under the hammer, then looked at Curley. I didn't quite yet understand what he'd said earlier about using supplies early to save supplies late, but I had decided to trust him, and trust him I would.

He gestured to the log. "Take a position."

I knelt behind the log and rested the rifle.

"See dat hat?"

"Yes, sir."

"I make it close to fifty yards. Take aim and see what you can do."

I looked up in question. "But it's your hat."

"Ne'er you mind about dat. There be some things more important than a hat." He waved his arm. "Line the sights onto your target." He pointed toward the hat. "Let's be seeing what you can do."

I shrugged, then settled in behind the rifle. The barrel, rock still, gave me hope. When I had lined up the sights, I pulled the trigger, fully expecting to see the hat fluttering to the ground, but it didn't move. I breathed out in frustration as I glanced up to Curley.

"Boy, you be jerking that trigger like you thought a cottonmouth was striking. When you jerk like that, it throws everything off. You has to be smooth. Don't get into a rush. Put pressure on the trigger slow until it breaks. Let the rifle do the work." He smiled. "That be your second lesson. Now, load up and take another shot."

I settled in again, determined to be gentle on the trigger. I took a deep breath in and held it while concentrating on the hat beyond the rifle's front sight. Before I pulled the trigger, I felt a hand on my shoulder. I relaxed my finger and looked up.

"You got to breathe, young'un. Holdin' your breath be making you less steady. Take a breath and let it out slow while you be pullin' just as slow on the trigger. I'm thinkin' that be lesson number three."

The trigger broke, the gun fired and I was hopeful but disappointed. His hat rested in the bush oblivious to my intentions of filling it full of holes. I frowned. Another ball wasted even though I was sure I'd done everything Curley had suggested.

I looked to him. "What am I doing wrong?"

He chuckled. "Ain't doing nothin' wrong. You only needs to learn the rifle. Just like folks, every one be different. Load up and try again."

The hammer dropped, the cap sent fire to the powder which sent the ball screaming out of the barrel. I opened my eyes, surprised to see the hat fluttering to the ground.

Behind me, Curley slapped his thigh. "That be the way. Slow and steady. That's what I always say. Slow and steady wins the race." He clapped me on my back. "That be some good shooting there."

I grinned at the compliment. I'd actually put the ball where I'd been aiming and I felt ten feet tall.

He held his hand over his eyes as he checked the position of the sun. "I gots to be getting back." He pointed to the rifle. "You load it again but don't set the cap. You can ride with me and hope to see something on the way." He winked then jogged to retrieve his hat. When he returned, he touched a hole in the crown and chuckled. "I've never been so proud of a hole in my hat."

I looked at the hole and felt the same way.

Chapter 6

Side by side we rode, he on a fine bay mare and me, bareback, on Old Jackson. Each step took me farther from my home, but I, unthinking, didn't notice. Curley talked and told stories and before I knew it, we rode onto the lane leading to the Grunwald's house. He pulled his mare to a stop, so I did likewise.

He leaned down in his saddle, resting his arm on the saddlehorn. "Mrs. Grunwald, she asks about you every now and again. Why don't you come on to the house and be telling her hello?"

I looked from him to the house, then turned to look behind at the path we had ridden. I shook my head and peered at him. At his smile, I could plainly see that Curley had deliberately led me to the house. He had told his stories and drawn me along like a hungry pup following scraps of meat. I suppose I should have been angry, but I wasn't. I remembered fondly the single meal I'd shared with the Grunwalds and the peaches Curley and I had eaten in the root cellar.

I grinned. "You done that on purpose, didn't you? Led me here like a lost calf."

His eyes opened wide in pretend shock, then he laughed. "I don't know what you be talking about." He kicked the mare toward the house. Old Jackson dropped his head and followed behind.

Curley rode directly to the front door and called in a booming voice, "Mrs. Grunwald? Mrs. Grunwald, young Branson Hawk has come a callin'."

The door opened, she stepped out and leaned against an awning post, holding her hand over her eyes to block the afternoon sun. She saw me and grinned. "Get down and come in, young man."

Curley dismounted and held his hand for the reins and the rifle. I passed them over and stepped onto the porch. She grabbed my arm and pushed me gently through the open door.

"I am so glad you could come visit." She motioned for me to take a chair, but my old coveralls were much too dirty to sit on one of the cushioned chairs in her parlor.

I took off my hat and stood, somewhat uncomfortable. "Thank you, ma'am, but I can't stay. I only stopped to tell you hello."

"Well, I'm glad you did. Let me find Gunther." She hurried into a hallway and called to the back of the house. "Gunther, Branson Hawk has come to call."

Within a minute, both stood in front of me. I shifted nervously from foot to foot while I twirled my hat in my hand.

Mr. Grunwald took his spectacles off, folded them and placed them into his coat pocket. He motioned to a chair but I shook my head. He nodded appreciation, then pulled the lapels of his coat. "Tell me, young Branson, how has your family been getting along?"

I dropped my head. "Not so good. Crop has burned up in

the field."

He frowned. "Yes, most everyone in these parts is having the same trouble. It's going to be a long summer if it doesn't start raining soon."

My lips pressed together. "Yes, sir." I couldn't say more. It was already a long summer for us. Even if it started raining right away, our crop was ruined.

"And your ma and pa?"

I swallowed. "Ma's fine." I was too embarrassed to mention anything about Pa.

After my answer, the stillness hung in the air. It was as though they could tell something was amiss, but were too polite to ask. They exchanged glances and I felt foolish. I wished Curley hadn't brought me.

I looked toward the door. "I'd best be going now. I've got a far piece to ride to get home before dark."

"Of course, of course." Mr. Grunwald led the way to the door and opened it to allow me to leave.

He followed me through and cleared his throat. "Branson?"

I took the reins from Curley, then turned. "Yes, sir?"

He looked to his wife and got a nod of approval. He smiled as he turned to me. "We have some chores here that Curley could use some help with. Reckon you could find time to help us out? I could pay."

Without thinking, I started to decline because I knew Pa would not allow it. I caught myself in instant realization that Pa no longer had a say in the matter, and that working for the Grunwalds might be our salvation. I could earn enough money to keep the family in necessities and groceries. It was an answer to our prayers.

"Yes, sir. I'd be proud to help out. I can come pert near anytime you need me."

"Splendid, splendid. Get here sometime after sunup tomorrow."

"I'll be here. Thank you, sir." I grabbed Jackson's mane and jumped, trying to get my belly high enough on the mule's back so I could shimmy up. I didn't quite make it but Curley leaned in his saddle to grab the back of my shirt and pull me on. When I was situated, he handed me the rifle which I balanced over the mule's withers. Before I could say thank you, Mr. Grunwald placed one hand on Jackson's neck and the other on my thigh.

"You still like bacon?"

I remembered the bacon he'd sent home that cold winter day a year and a half earlier. "Yes, sir."

He gestured toward the house. "If you'll wait for half a minute, Henrietta has gone to fetch you some from the root cellar. We'll call it an advance on your wages."

I noticed for the first time that she was gone. I saw Curley's smile and couldn't help but join him. A mite of bacon would taste mighty good alongside the mush I was sure we'd be eating that night. My mouth watered at the thought.

"You are too kind, sir."

"Nonsense. Payment for work to be done."

Mrs. Grunwald hurried through the door carrying a parcel tied in a gunny sack. She stepped down from the porch and passed it up. I held it clumsily, trying to balance it along with the rifle. There was no way I'd be able to get both home.

Curley reached for the bacon and held it on his saddle horn. He leaned toward Mr. Grunwald. "Begging your permission, sir, I'll ride along with the boy to see him safe home."

"Splendid, splendid."

Dusk was upon the prairie when, after taking care of Jackson and bidding Curley goodbye, I stepped into the house. I leaned the rifle against the wall and placed the sack on the table. Ma wiped her hands on her apron with a questioning look.

I patted the meat. "The Grunwalds want me to work for them a few days a week. They sent this as payment for work to be done."

She sighed and I didn't know if it was a sigh of relief or one of despair. She stepped away from the stove and the boiling pot of mush. Silently, she reached for a hug and while squeezing me tightly, kissed the top of my head.

"I'm sorry you have to do this." She stepped back and lifted my face with a hand under my chin. "Thank you."

I noticed for the first time that her face seemed thinner and more drawn than only the day before, and her red-rimmed eyes only served to increase my love for her. She wiped her eyes with her fingers then turned again to the stove.

We ate bacon that night around a gloomy table. Josiah and Myrtle asked repeatedly where Pa was, their young minds not understanding that Pa was gone and we were left to fend for ourselves. It was a depressing night, one of many to come.

The next morning I bridled Jackson and pushed him to the fence so I could step on the rails and slip onto his back. I reached for the rifle I'd leaned against the fence, then kicked the mule into a steady walk toward the Grunwald's.

When I got to my destination, Curley called me to the barn where he handed me a brush. and currycomb. We worked together cleaning the horses while he told stories. I listened attentively, not realizing at the time that every story had a moral and that he, in his way, was trying to teach me.

I stopped and leaned on a sorrel mare. "Curley, where are all of the servants?"

"Servants?"

"Hired folks. I thought all rich folks had servants and such."

He laughed. "Mr. and Mrs. Grunwald be regular folk. He

makes an honest living on his land, and I'm the only hired man, except for the planting and harvesting crews in the spring and fall." He grinned. "Least ways, I was the only hired man until you showed up."

Time marched on. The days grew shorter as summer faded into fall, fall to winter and winter to early spring. I spent three days a week at the Grunwalds working with Curley and the rest of my time helping Ma around our dugout cabin or hunting in the breaks a mile away. After a few more practice sessions with Curley, my ability with the rifle improved to the point that we had a steady supply of meat to go along with food from Mrs. Grunwald's garden. They paid me in food each week because, as I came to learn, the war was hard on everyone.

Every Saturday we hitched Jackson to the rickety wagon and made a trip to the post office in Lawrence. Every Saturday Ma came from the building with a false, forced smile and I knew that no letter, and no money, had arrived from Pa. She would then take us to the store where we would do nothing more than browse because we couldn't buy anything. I wondered then if the store visits were only an attempt to hide the actual reason for our weekly visit to town.

I had turned thirteen, and as Ma had reminded me many times, life on the prairie, especially life on the prairie without a pa, made a boy grow up faster than the Good Lord intended. As much as we didn't want to admit it, our chances of ever seeing any money of Pa's soldier pay grew less each week. If we were to make it, we'd have to make it on our own. I wasn't a kid any longer and had talked with her about planting our fields. Since I was the man of the house, I wanted to give it a try. I could plow and Ma and Caleb could plant. If the rains were good we could harvest a crop and make enough money to see us through.

The early spring chased the last chill of winter from

Eastern Kansas. We sat in our wagon on that Saturday with renewed hope because of the warmth in the air, but after another disappointing visit to the post office, Ma pasted the pretend smile on her face and took us to the store to talk to Mr. Smithson about giving us enough credit for seed. He had helped in the past and we had every reason to think he would again. I led the family into the store with every intention of asking for the loan, but stopped as the store was crowded with several folks gathered at the counter discussing the war. We stood close and listened, disappointed and fearful at the news that the Confederate army was in the north and that the war, rather than the short event all expected, had turned into a drawn out conflict with no end in sight. All thoughts of seed corn left at the disheartening news.

The conversation turned to the marauders from Missouri who came with increasing regularity to Eastern Kansas in the name of the Confederate army. With fearful faces, men and women in the group told of the plundering, rape and murder in the countryside. We knew, of course, of the earlier instances of pro-slavery mobs who'd raided the countryside and once burned our little town, but that was before the war. This was the first we'd heard of the new threat.

Mr. Smithson, the storeowner, raised to his full height. "They aren't soldiers. They are only outlaws taking advantage of the war and using it for an excuse to do their dirty work."

The crowd murmured their agreement.

Ma leaned in. "Where exactly do these marauders target?"

The owner rubbed his hands on the wooden counter. "Mostly to places away from town where there is something to steal."

Ma and I exchanged glances. We had nothing to steal, but our place was away from town, secluded and away from any roads or trails. With heads down, we left the store and loaded in the wagon. I glanced one time at Ma, then slapped the reins on Old Jackson. He leaned into the collar and our run-down wagon creaked as it rolled out of town.

Caleb and the twins lounged in the back. Ma glanced over her shoulder before leaning to me.

"I've been thinking, Branson. If there are marauders in these parts, maybe it would be best if you stayed closer to the house for a while."

I nodded. I'd been thinking the same thing. I would miss the opportunity to work with Curley. I enjoyed his company and the things I'd been learning. Other than family, he was the only friend I had. Still, it would be best to pay attention to any strangers headed our way. I could hunt close to the house and keep an eye out. We could get by.

The early spring continued with welcome, warm weather. I realized that in not too many weeks, the coolness of spring would give way to the heat of summer, but for the time being, we enjoyed the pleasant days.

I left in the night's remaining blackness in hopes of finding meat. Gray light from the eastern sky spread over the flat land slowly pushing the blanket of darkness away. I licked my thumb and rubbed the front sight of the rifle like Curley had shown me. I don't know if it did any good, but it had become a ritual of sorts whenever I got ready to shoot. A flock of wild turkeys grazed toward me, coming closer each minute. I'd heard them in the predawn stillness so I hunkered down to wait to see if they would show themselves. I was afoot, having left Old Jackson for Caleb to use to gather wood. Our cabin was only three quarters of a mile behind me and I'd promised Ma that I would stay within a mile in case we had any unwelcome visitors. If all went well, I expected to be back long before midmorning with something for our table.

The prairie grass kept the turkeys from my view, but I knew by their sounds that they were steadily getting closer. I rested the long barrel of the rifle over a woody shrub, pointing to where I expected them to appear. I grinned as they approached and I could see four toms and a dozen hens. I took aim at one of the younger toms and slowly squeezed the trigger.

The rifle fired and my quarry staggered while the others loudly took flight. I stood with a grin on my face, proud of my increasing ability with the rifle. I could see the wounded turkey thrashing in the grass so I jogged there, never taking my eyes from the spot because I knew that in the tall grass, a dead bird could blend in so well that it would be almost impossible to find unless I knew exactly where to go.

The thrashing stopped as I got closer, but with a whoosh, the turkey rose into the air and unsteadily flew a hundred yards. I growled to myself as I sprinted toward his landing place. He was mortally wounded, of that I was sure, but I would have to keep pace with him if I hoped to find him when he could fly no longer.

Several times, the determined bird took flight at my approach, although each time the distance diminished. He took me deeper into the breaks and by the time he finally breathed his last and I was able to gather him up, I was no less than a mile and a half away from our dugout. I was winded, but I'd promised Ma to stay close, so I tucked the bird under my arm and jogged toward home.

The orange ball of the sum climbed from the horizon and I was tired from all the running. I wanted to stop and rest and decided I would get my chance when I topped the next high spot and could look down on our homestead. As I grew closer to the resting place, I thought I heard screaming. My eyes opened wide and I dropped the turkey to sprint the last few yards. I took a sharp breath when I saw three mounted men riding circles around the dugout. Ma stood at the door, throwing whatever she could get her hands on at the men. I realized it was her screaming that I'd heard. One of the men stopped and dismounted, rushing the door and reaching for her. In no time he had dragged her to his horse. Caleb ran from the cabin but went down in a heap when another man pointed a pistol and shot. Ma somehow kicked free and tumbled to the ground, then ran to Caleb and fell across his chest.

It happened so fast and I was too far away. I jerked a percussion cap from my bag and set it to my rifle, thankful that I had charged and loaded it after running down the turkey. I threw the gun to my shoulder and snapped off a shot. I was much too far away to have any hope of hitting one of the men, but perhaps knowing they were targets would send them scurrying away.

The shot did exactly that. They looked toward me and spurred their horses, but not before shooting their pistols and throwing their torches into the dugout. They rode past the corral and barn and it was only then that I noticed a fourth rider on a paint horse leading Jackson away. The men caught up then whipped the mule into keeping pace with the galloping horses.

I ran to the cabin, afraid of what I'd find. When I got there, it was worse than I'd feared. Ma lay over Caleb, but she'd been shot in the back. I rolled her over, hoping for any sign of life and caught my breath as her eyes fluttered. I looked into her face, noticing blood on her mouth and when I tried to wipe it away, she shook her head and spit something out. I realized then that she had bitten the vile man's finger completely off and that was likely how she'd been able to escape his clutches.

I tenderly wiped the hair from her face, then pulled the dress that had been ripped from her shoulders to cover her nakedness. I gritted my teeth at the unrestrained evil of the men.

"I'm sorry, Ma. I should have been here."

She peered at me through pain-filled eyes. "It wasn't your

fault." Her voice was only a whisper and I had to lean close to hear.

I put my finger to her lips. "Don't talk, Ma. Save your strength."

She shook her head ever so slightly. "It's up to you now, Branson. I hid the twins in my hope chest at the foot of the bed. Take care of them."

I braved a look at the burning cabin and knew they had not survived. Even away from the cabin as we were, I could only look at the fire for a few seconds before being forced to lower my head so my hat brim would block the heat.

"I will, Ma. I will." I took the tiniest comfort as she forced a thin smile at my lie.

She immediately cringed in pain. When the wave passed, she opened her eyes again and I was shocked at the intensity of the blue color. I had not noticed until that moment just how blue her eyes were.

"And Caleb. They shot him for no reason."

"I know, Ma. I'll take care of him too." Tears dripped from my nose as I looked down to her. She was a good woman and didn't deserve what she got.

Her eyes closed for the last time and she lay limp in my arms. I pulled her close to my chest and wailed in grief. It had been my fault. If I hadn't chased the turkey so far into the breaks, I might have been close enough to help.

I held her tightly, breathing in the smell of her hair and feeling the warmth of her body. I longed to tell her how much I loved her and to apologize that I hadn't been there to protect her. Tears filled my eyes and my breath caught in my throat. I wanted to hold her for a long time, but I had other things that needed done. I let her limp body slide away so I could attend to Caleb, but the hole in the center of his chest and his open, lifeless eyes told me there was nothing I could do. I held my arm over my face to block the heat as I looked toward the cabin. Flames shot through the door as every wooden thing inside burned with tremendous ferocity, and I hoped that Josiah and Myrtle had not suffered too much.

I stood and staggered away, then sank to my knees. My entire family was gone, my whole world torn apart. The grief overwhelmed me and I rolled to my side in the dirt. I cried for a long time with no effort to restrain the gasping sobs of regret and sorrow.

At length I rolled to sit on the dirt, my crying finished, my tears exhausted. As I sat there, the feeling of loss in my chest slowly made room for another emotion. Hate. I'd never known hate before, but I knew it then. I had no idea who the marauders were, but the time would come for them to pay for what they'd done.

The hate moved me to action. I carried Caleb and Ma to a hole Pa and I had dug for our root cellar. It was another of Pa's grand plans that never got finished, but it would make a decent grave. I covered the bodies with the dirt mounded at the sides, then I made a cross out of some planks from the barn and pushed it deep into the soft earth. That finished, I gathered my rifle and started the long walk to the Grunwalds, for I had nowhere else to go.

Curley saw me coming. I don't know how he did it, but he always seemed to know if anyone was close by, and I suspected he was paying extra close attention because of the threat of marauders. He strode toward me, then hurried his pace when he saw my condition. As he approached, I lost all strength and fell against this chest.

"Glory be, Branson. What happened to you?" He scooped me into his arms and carried me to the front door while calling loudly for Mrs. Grunwald.

She and her husband met us at the door. She stood back motioning for Curley to lay me on a rug. Curley took the rifle while Mrs. Grunwald felt at my chest with her hand. She looked to Curley. "Has he been shot?"

I hadn't been shot and couldn't understand why she

would ask such a question.

Curley knelt beside me and ripped my shirt away. "No ma'am. His shirt is bloody, that's all."

I realized then that it was Ma's blood. I tried to sit up so I could explain.

Curley reached a thick hand and pulled me forward to sit on the floor. "What happened, Branson?"

The pain in my chest returned at the question. I took a breath and swallowed, slowly looking in turn at the three faces that peered at me with concern. "Marauders."

Mrs. Grunwald held her hand to her mouth. "And your family?"

I slowly shook my head and choked back a whine. "All dead."

Her eyes opened wide. "No!"

I looked at her dumbly, wishing it was not so, but it was. I looked to Mr. Grunwald, then to Curley. "I'll get 'em. I'll track them down and kill every last one of them."

Mr. Grunwald spoke for the first time. "No. The law will catch up to them sooner or later. There's no reason for you to get yourself killed too. You've been through a terrible experience. You're welcome to stay with us for as long as you like."

I stared at him. He obviously didn't know the heartache I felt. I didn't care so much about where I might stay, rather, I wanted to take after the marauders and make them pay. I slowly shook my head, then turned my attention to Curley. He would understand. He knew the pain of losing a family. He returned my gaze with sorrowful eyes.

"Curley, you'll help me won't you?"

He glanced quickly at the man and woman, then considered me. "Lawd's sake, Branson. Mr. Grunwald is right. Them be growed men who don't think twice about killing. They won't take into account that you is just a boy."

I, after the day's events, knew better than anyone that the

marauders had no reservations when it came to killing, but my mind was made up, with or without help. My eyes narrowed and I started to rise. If they wouldn't help me, I'd do it on my own. I wasn't a child any longer. I had aged considerable in the last twelve hours.

Curley placed a huge hand on my shoulder, holding me down. I wanted to protest, to throw his hand from me so I could leave, but I noticed a look of compassion in his eyes, along with what I took to be a warning not to do anything foolish. I relaxed because with his weight on me I wasn't going anywhere anyway. He nodded, moved his hand to my wrist and pulled me to my feet and into his arms.

If the Grunwalds were surprised at his show of affection, they didn't show it. Curley and I had become good friends during my time working there. We shared in the work and he had spent hours talking to me, sharing experiences and teaching me with stories. I suppose the Grunwalds had accepted our bonding and thought no more of it.

Curley patted my back, released his grip and held me at arm's length to look into my eyes. "You rest up here with Mr. and Mrs. Grunwald for a time. I know how you be feeling right now, and I also know that time is the only healer. You stay and work with me to keep your mind off your troubles."

I took a deep breath and nodded. I saw the wisdom in waiting for a few days at least. I could bide my time. Besides, I had nowhere else to go and I needed a plan. I could stay for a while and make preparations. After that, no matter what the Grunwalds or Curley said, I'd go after the men who'd killed my family. I wouldn't rest until they were dead.

I took a step back and looked into each of their faces. "Thank you."

Mrs. Grunwald clapped her hands under her chin. "Come to the kitchen for something to eat?"

I shook my head. After what had happened that day, I had no appetite.

Curley stepped forward. "Go on in. You have to keep your strength up even if you don't feel like eatin'."

I reluctantly followed her and took the bowl of beef stew from her hands. I ate two helpings, not so much because I was starving, but because of what Curley had said. I did need to keep and build my strength. I would need it when the time came to light out after the marauders.

Dusk came and went. I had stayed in the house with the Grunwalds and I hadn't seen Curley since following Mrs. Grunwald into the kitchen. The hours slipped by as I sat in a cushioned chair, rocking slowly, alone in the formal parlor room. My thoughts were of my family and I grieved again. In truth, I suspected that was the reason The Grunwalds and Curley had left me alone.

Mrs. Grunwald entered holding a flannel nightshirt. She handed it to me and bade me rise from the chair. "Follow me."

She led through the house to a room in the back and pointed to the bed. "You can sleep here."

I looked into her kind face. "Thank you, ma'am."

She touched my shoulder. "Branson, you can stay with us as long as you like. We never had youngsters. It will be nice to have a young man in the house."

I looked at her blankly, not knowing exactly what to do or what to say. I was happy she didn't wait for any conversation from me.

"And tomorrow, Gunther will ride to town to tell the marshal about what happened at your place."

The mention brought the smoldering hate to the surface. I had no confidence that the law would do anything, especially with us being poor folk. No, if anything was to be done, I would have to do it myself.

Randall Dale

Chapter 7

It was a long and restless night and I thought the sun would never show itself again. But it did, and with it a renewed hope on my part that I would be able to find the killers. I slipped out of the house as soon as it got light enough to see. As expected, Curley was feeding the horses, forking prairie hay from the loft into the mangers. When I entered the barn, he folded his arms over the handle of the pitchfork and looked down on me with a solemn expression.

"Morning, Branson." He thrust the fork into a pile of hay then climbed down the ladder to stand in front of me. "Get any sleep?"

I shook my head as I looked up into his face. "Not more'n a few hours at best."

He placed a heavy hand on my shoulder, then peered over my head to the big door. Satisfied that Mr. or Mrs. Grunwald had not followed me, he turned to sit on a grain sack while pulling me to sit at his side.

"I knows how you feel and I don't blame you."

His voice was soft, barely more than a whisper, but I

hoped I heard in it a willingness to help. I sat straight. "Will you help me?"

He remained quiet, sitting without speaking for a long time as he looked out the barn doors to the graying landscape. At length he turned to me. "First things first. You can't be saying a word to Mr. and Mrs. Grunwald about our planning to go after the killers. Do you promise?"

"Yes, sir. I won't say a word."

His smile was tight, without humor. "And will you agree to go slow and steady?"

If he was offering help, I would have expected to start out after the marauders while their trail was fresh. Anybody with any common sense would know that. I frowned. "We don't have time to waste. They already have a day's head start. If we expect to catch them, we need to leave right away."

He shook his big head. "No. The first thing we'd best be doing is getting information."

"Information?"

"Yes. Who was they and where they be from?"

I tapped my foot on the barn floor. "Who cares what their names are or where they are from?"

He took a deep breath then looked at me with hard eyes. "I do, for one."

My eyes narrowed. "What difference does it make?"

As he studied me it seemed as if his eyes bored right through and I realized that whether I agreed or not, we would do things his way. I had never chased a man and although I talked a big story, I didn't know the first thing about hunting down killers. I dropped my head. "All right, all right. We'll do it your way. I only hope it won't be too long."

He grunted. "Slow and steady, slow and steady."

Over the next few months my patience grew raw as I learned that slow and steady actually meant almost constant inaction as it dealt with finding the marauders. But farm work went on. I worked with the plowing and planting crew hired by Mr. Grunwald and felt pride that at barely thirteen, I had been valuable help. When they left, Curley and I took care of the crops, the garden and whatever else needed tending. Summer passed and fall came, and with it the harvest crew where I helped again, then Mrs. Grunwald demanded I go to school for winter and spring. I complied while looking forward every day to the time Curley and I would take out after the marauders.

In between working and school, Curley tried to teach me things I'd need to know when and if the time ever came to hunt down the men who'd murdered my family. He taught me about tracking, about concealment and about stalking. We practiced with our rifles and he gave me a knife with a scabbard which I wore at my side, but the teaching moments, while beneficial, were too sporadic, and school only seemed to hamper the most important learning I wanted to undertake. My impatience could not be hidden, but no matter how much I wanted to spend my time with Curley, there was no way Mrs. Grunwald would allow me to quit school. I smothered my exasperation because Curley never wavered from his slow and steady approach and Mrs. Grunwald made sure that school was never missed.

That all changed the summer before I turned fifteen. The long desired growth spurt stretched my bones. I had grown to a man's height and could look Curley square in the eye. My shoulders, though not as broad as his, had grown thicker with the hard work and good food, and my muscles stretched the fabric of my shirts.

Curley, in good-natured teasing, had started the previous summer, a habit of throwing me into the water trough between the house and the barn. It was all in fun and I enjoyed the wrestling, and in truth, didn't mind cooling off after a hot day of work.

That fateful summer day had been hot and the sweat rolled from our faces as we drove the teams home from a day of cultivating the corn fields. When we had taken care of the horses, Curley wiped the sweat from his brow.

"Glory be. I don't know as I've ever been so hot."

I nodded, then started toward the hand pump and water trough to wash for supper. We walked through the barn door and as we approached the trough, I grabbed the handle to pump water for him to wash his face. With catlike quickness, he jerked my arm and tried to pick me up to throw me into the trough, but I was ready. I had been waiting for a chance to pay him back. I ducked under his arm and with one arm between his legs and the other around his waist, I grunted and strained to pick him up and bury him into the water. He held tight to me and pulled me in also, but there was no denying I had won the battle.

I pushed up and away from the trough to stand at the side with a huge grin. It was the first time I'd bested him and I rejoiced in the accomplishment. I had no pretenses that I'd be able to do it again because it was only in surprise that I had prevailed. His face came sputtering out of the water and he shook his head, flinging tiny droplets of water from his close-cropped hair. He looked at me with a serious expression, studying me as though he was seeing me for the first time. He rubbed his hand over his face and down his scraggly beard, then leaned back with both arms stretched over the side of the trough as he sat on the bottom. He cocked his head as he continued to stare, then he nodded.

"Tonight," was all he said.

"What's tonight?"

He stood in the trough and stepped over the side, rubbing his face again and flicking the water from his hands. He didn't speak again, but went straight to his shack beyond the root cellar. I watched him go before turning into the house.

The Grunwalds and I sat at the fancy table eating a fancy supper, but my thoughts were with Curley. As I replayed the events at the water trough, especially his leaving without his customary smile, I wondered if I'd made him mad. He had always held the upper hand, but in that brief moment, I was king of the hill. Still, I knew my victory was temporary. The man was stronger than a bull ox at least twice as broad in the chest as me. He undoubtedly would be ready if I was to try it again. I gazed into my soup, absently stirring with the silver spoon as I thought of the man I so admired.

I slowly came to the realization that Mr. and Mrs. Grunwald had stopped eating. I glanced up to see them staring at me.

Mrs. Grunwald leaned forward. "Branson, is there anything wrong?"

"No, ma'am. I was only thinking about Curley."

"What about Curley."

There were so many questions I wanted to ask. The man was my friend, my only friend, but I knew so little about him. I wanted to know how he'd escaped his earlier life of slavery to come to work for the Grunwalds. I wanted to know how he knew so much about the things he tried to teach me. And I wanted to know why was he so afraid of dogs. I looked up, somehow coming to the understanding that the story was his to tell, and it would be wrong for me to ask them. Someday I would ask him directly. Someday.

I looked into each of their faces. "Why doesn't Curley eat with us?"

Mr. Grunwald wiped his mouth with a cloth napkin, then placed it on the table and rested his chin on his clasped hands. He took a breath. "When he first came, we invited him every meal, but he always refused. He's never eaten a meal in this house, not a single one." He leaned back with both hands flat on the table. He glanced at his wife. "I reckon our asking made him uncomfortable, so over time we quit inviting him."

I nodded, happy to know the choice of not eating in the

house had been Curley's and had nothing to do with the color of his skin. I knew that Negroes, even free ones, were more often than not treated unkindly, and the folks in the anti-slavery town of Lawrence were seldom better.

Curley was a good man, and in many ways was more of a father to me than my own Pa had been. I regretted my lifting him into the trough and making him mad. I resolved then to apologize the next time I saw him.

After supper, with lantern in hand, I retreated to my room. I turned to close the door, then jumped in fright when a man stood from sitting on my bed. In the dim light of the lantern, I could see only the whites of his eyes.

"Curley?"

"Come with me, Branson."

He pushed past me through the door and down the hall to the back door of the house. I followed quickly, confused at where we might be going in the dark.

As he stepped out the door, he turned. "Blow out the lantern and leave it inside."

I cupped my hand over the chimney and blew the flame. With the light gone, darkness closed around me. I blinked, trying to get used to the blackness.

"Follow me."

He moved ghostlike with no sound and I struggled to keep up. After only a few yards, he was gone, so I stopped. "Curley? Curley, where are you?"

I jumped again when he tapped my shoulder. I turned and could only make out a shadow of his form, then he was gone again. My eyes slowly adjusted to the darkness and I found that if I kept low, I could make out his shape against the star-filled sky. As he walked away, I hunkered down and followed to the barn where I saw him slip through the door. I paused, unsure of what to do, then I saw the instant flare of a match, and increasing light as he lit a lantern and positioned the globe.

He waved me inside, but I hesitated at the lack of his ever-present smile. Perhaps he was madder than I thought at my afternoon frolicking. He motioned with his head again so I entered and followed him to the back of the barn where he placed the lantern on a post and leaned against the wall.

I raised my hands to shoulder height and opened my palms, then looked to him as he stared at me. "I'm sorry I put you in the trough this afternoon, Curley. I won't do it again."

He shook his head. "You think I be mad?"

I shrugged. What else could it be? The entire time I'd known him, his lips were rarely without a smile, yet, since the dunking, the smile was gone and his nature had turned serious. "Are you?"

He slowly shook his head. "I've been waiting for you to show me you are big enough, strong enough and old enough to learn what I have to teach you. You've growed, Branson Hawk. You ain't a young'un no more."

I pursed my lips and held my eyebrows down in confusion. "But you've been teaching when you could."

He nodded. "That be the truth, but now it's time for man-teaching."

Man-teaching? I cocked my head. I didn't know what that could mean, but I liked the sound of it. I also felt relief that he wasn't mad. I stepped closer. "I'm ready."

He pointed to the sacks, inviting me to sit with him there. When we were situated, he folded his arms and leaned against the wall. "You ever kill a man?"

He knew I'd never killed anyone because I'd been living with him and the Grunwalds since that awful day. I wondered at the question. "No."

"But you been thinking about it?"

I nodded. It had been my one thought for the past two years. Countless times I had imagined the men's deaths at my hands. Shooting, knifing or beating them with fists. It didn't matter the method, what mattered was accomplishing my desire.

"Yes, sir. Been thinking about it a lot."

"Easier to think about than to do it. You think you'll be happy when you're finished?"

I frowned at his questions. Of course I'd be happy. I had dreamed about the killing. In my thoughts, I had seen their faces as a bullet drove into their chests. I hoped they would recognize me and know the reason for tracking them down. I wanted them to pay, up close and personal, for what they'd done to my family. My eyes squinted. "I'll be more than happy."

"You'll enjoy it then? The killing I mean?"

"Oh yes, I'm going to enjoy it. I'll make them pay and laugh at their dying breath."

Curley dropped his head and looked down at his folded arms. He seemed to be ignoring me. He asked no further questions and made no additional comments until a full five minutes later when he stood and pointed toward the house. "You go on to bed, but meet me back here before light tomorrow and every day after." He pulled the lantern from the post, cupped his hand and blew out the flame, causing the instant darkness to close around me with an uncomfortable embrace.

I stood. "Curley, I can't see." I waited for a moment but soon realized that Curley had gone as soundlessly as the smoke from the lantern.

My dreams that night were uncomfortable. I dreamed of shooting one of the men and watching him die an agonizing death. In the dream, I welcomed his suffering and when he finally died, I laughed. Curley immediately appeared and glared at me with the same expression he'd used when he stood from the sacks. He was somehow disappointed in me, and it hurt.

I walked to the barn in the pre-dawn darkness holding the lantern high above my head so I could see. Curley waited for me. He sat on a sack, face set hard, ankles crossed and arms folded as he leaned against the wall. When I approached, he held his hand for the lantern. When I passed it to him, he blew the flame. The darkness, as the night before, was complete. I leaned forward to feel for the sacks so I could take a seat.

His deep voice cut through the gloom. "Branson Hawk, you showed yesterday that you be a man in size. Your muscles are strong and you've growed." He paused. "But size and muscles don't make the man. That be your first lesson."

I heard him stand from the sacks and I was confused. Was that all he had to say? He had promised to start the man-teaching, but he'd not taught anything of value when it came to tracking down the marauders. I stood from my sack. "Curley?"

"Yes."

I was shocked when his voice came from the barn door thirty feet away. I hadn't heard so much as a whisper of his clothes or a scratch in the dirt from one of his boots. "Is that all?"

"That be more than you can handle right now. I'm a thinking maybe you aren't as ready as I thought."

His confessions frightened me. He'd said he would teach me, but now it seemed as though he'd changed his mind.

"But I am ready."

"We'll see."

He didn't sound convinced and I was sure he was leaving. I took a step toward the door. "Teach me, Curley. You promised you would."

No sound came and my head and shoulders slumped, then I heard a downcast grunt. I looked, unseeing, toward the sound and felt disappointment at his change. To my profound relief, the voice came.

"Starting today you won't use a lantern. You must welcome the darkness, make it your friend, use it as a helper.

Never look directly at a light. If you are on the trail and set up camp with a fire, never be sittin' and lookin' into the flames. Always sit with your back to the fire so your eyes be used to the dark."

"Yes sir. I'll do that. Anything else?"

Silence. He had gone.

Chapter 8

I cultivated in the fields all that day, alone and thoughtful. I didn't know where Curley had gone and concluded he simply didn't want to be with me that day. I remembered the dream and the disappointment in Curley's eyes when I laughed. My mind wandered until in my remembrance, I stood again at the high spot above our cabin and I could hear the marauder's pistols as they shot Caleb and Ma. I shuddered as I thought of the men who'd taken so much from me, then in my imagination, I heard them laugh in cold-hearted glee at the death they'd caused.

When I returned to the barn that evening, I caught only a passing glimpse at Curley. He looked toward me with no expression. He simply turned and walked away. I took care of the mule then washed at the trough before supper. I walked to where I'd seen Curley, searching for the man, anxious to make amends, to see his smiling face and hear his constant banter, but he was not to be found.

The next morning, long before the rising of the sun, I made my way in the dark to the barn and found the sacks. I climbed up to sit, then nearly jumped out of my skin when he spoke.

"Morning, Branson."

My heart raced as I held my hand to my face. I took a deep breath to calm my jangled nerves. "Curley, you scared the living daylights out of me."

"What did you learn?"

What did I learn? What kind of question was that? I'd learned that with him sitting there so still, he surprised me, that's what I'd learned. I told him so.

He was quiet for a long moment and I found that if I was also silent, I could hear his faint breathing. His earlier teaching surfaced and I remembered his numerous lessons in stalking, how I would need to still myself, to calm myself in order to listen for any sound that might tell me the whereabouts of the man or beast being tracked. I nodded in the dark, suddenly aware that he waited for me to come to the conclusion.

"I learned that I should have been still and silent."

I heard him take a deep breath and let it out, and I knew he'd done it loud enough for me to hear so I would know that my answer had been correct. I smiled in the dark.

We sat in silence for a few minutes, and in those minutes I concentrated on making no sound. I refrained from movement and kept my breath slow and shallow. He had done the same.

When he next spoke, his voice was strong and forceful. "Tell me again how you will feel when you kill a man."

I rubbed my face with both hands as I remembered the thoughts I'd had the previous day. I was embarrassed at what I'd said to Curley about laughing at the dying breaths of the marauders. I looked down with a frown and nervously picked at my fingers. "I've been thinking about that. I still want them to pay for what they've done, and if that payment is made by death at my hand, I will not shed a tear. They chose their path as I have chosen mine, but," I paused, "but I won't be laughing. If I did, I would be no better than them."

Silence again in the big barn until I heard him slap his thigh. "Mr. Branson Hawk," a deep chuckle escaped his throat, "now I can see you is ready."

His perpetual smile and pleasant banter returned that day and continued in the days and weeks that followed. We met in the barn each morning before sunrise and his teaching grew more pressing. It was as if he wanted me to know all he knew and that his time for teaching was limited.

We spent hours on the prairie with me tracking him and him tracking me He took special pains to teach the finer points of concealment and stalking. I learned fast, for I had a good reason. Though he never said it in so many words, I could feel that my time for hunting the raiders who'd killed my family drew closer each day.

"Go to the root cellar and get me a bottle of peaches." He made the request early one morning as the gray of dawn slowly overtook the darkness. Weeks had grown to months and with his teaching, my confidence was high that I'd be able to avenge the loss of my family. I stood from the sacks where we sat. It seemed an odd thing for him to ask. He'd never done it before, but I hustled out of the barn and to the cellar, then came jogging back with a bottle of peaches in my hand.

He took them and motioned for me to sit again on the sack.

"What did you see on the way to the cellar?"

I turned and looked out the barn door. Seen? I hadn't seen anything. He'd asked for me to get peaches so that's what I did. I turned back to him.

His face grew serious. "What did you see?"

I shrugged. "Didn't see anything. Only went to the cellar like you asked."

"You didn't see the horse collar hanging from the clothesline post?"

I frowned. "Why would a horse collar be hanging there?"

His eyebrows raised and he tilted his head. "How about the rifle leaning against the back door of the house? You walked right past it on your way to the cellar."

I tried to picture the house and my jog to the cellar. I was certain there had been no rifle there. I was confused. Why the questions? I opened my mouth to speak but stopped and leaned back on the sack. Curley was teaching me something, but I couldn't' discern exactly what it was he had on his mind.

I sat quietly, waiting for him. He silently gazed at me for a full minute, then swung his legs from the sacks and stood. He motioned with his head for me to follow. At the clothesline, he paused and pointed. Just as he had said, a horse collar with brass knobs hung on the post. I hadn't seen it, although it had of a certain been there when I walked by. But, I reasoned, why would I look at it? It had nothing to do with me. I smiled and raised my palms, but his serious expression never changed.

Without a word, he walked toward the root cellar, but paused at the back door of the house. He reached and grasped the long rifle leaning there. He ignored me as he studied the rifle, turning it over in his hands. Finally, he looked to me and handed me the gun. I felt its heaviness while realizing I'd stepped within a foot of it as I hurried to the cellar.

Slowly, his teaching made sense. It wasn't about the rifle or the collar, they were only objects for his lesson. I had failed to notice either even though they were glaringly out of place. His dark eyes rested on me and I could feel his disapproval. He was trying to teach me what I would need to know to go after the marauders and in my pride I had felt I knew enough. I dropped my head in shame.

Additional weeks followed, one after the other, and I, with a renewed desire to learn more, did. We spent time in the woods playing hide and seek and few were the times he was able to evade me. Each day Curley asked me questions about what I'd seen and in time my noticing my surroundings became second nature. I had learned so much and it seemed the only thing to do now was find out who the raiders had been and go after them.

Our early morning meetings continued. On those dark mornings we talked of what he'd learned about the marauders. I don't know where he got his information, for I never saw anyone come to the farm and he never left that I could see, but over the months, morsel by morsel, the tidbits of information began to solidify.

He learned that the group of marauders hailed from Missouri and were led by a glorified outlaw by the name of Quantrill who fancied himself as a Confederate Captain and had taken the self-appointed task of making Kansans suffer for siding with the Union. He led a motley but large group of lawless men on raids in eastern Kansas, always moving from place to place to keep from getting caught. The band plundered, raped and murdered almost at will because local lawmen had not the will or the ability to chase and capture such a large band, and no soldiers were available because of the fighting in the east. Every day Curley drew a map of Kansas on the dirt floor, poking a stick to show me where they had last attacked.

Early one morning, Curley waited for me as I entered the barn. He sat on the feed sacks and invited me to join him there. He rubbed his jaw, then folded his arms. "I learnt that it wasn't Quantrill what killed your family."

I frowned. "I thought you said it was."

He nodded slowly. "I did, and when I say it wasn't Quantrill, what I mean is that it wasn't the main group, but some of his men who broke away and started raiding on their own."

I slapped my thigh. "That's why there were only four of

them."

"That's right."

I grew anxious. Four men instead of thirty, or fifty or even a hundred was much more possible. "What else did you learn?"

"Only that they are getting braver, making raids around this country while Quantrill is back in Missouri."

I tapped my knees with my fingers, imagining the time when I would meet them and make them pay. I looked to Curley. "When can we go after them?"

He exhaled in exasperation. "You sure be in an awful hurry to get yourself killed."

I pursed my lips and took a deep breath. "But it's been more'n two years and I've learned so much."

His eyes burned holes as he stared at me.

I leaned back and raised my palms. "I know, I know." I shook my head. "Slow and steady wins the race."

He nodded. "And the last thing is that there are only three of them now."

I blinked. "Why's that?"

He didn't answer, he only shrugged.

Late summer came to the Grunwald farm with tall, tasseled corn plants waving in the breeze. Mr. Grunwald sat in the buggy with a classy sorrel mare at the end of the reins. He gazed at the fields and smiled before looking down at Curley and me as we stood alongside the buggy.

"Possibly one of the finest crops we've ever had here, wouldn't you say, Curley?"

"Yes, sir. You be one of the best farmers in all of Kansas."

Mr. Grunwald smirked. "Curley, you know I'm not the farmer. You do the work and you manage the crews when they come to plow, plant and harvest. I'm beholding to you."

Curley looked away as though the comment had embarrassed him. He scratched at the black earth next to the buggy with his boot. "It be me who is beholdin' to you and the missus. I'll ne'er be able to repay you for your kindness all them years ago."

I watched the interaction with surprise. I had heard them constantly banter back and forth in good-natured teasing, but they'd never spoken to each other with the honest sincerity I witnessed, at least not anytime I was around. I wondered at the reason Curley was indebted to Mr. and Mrs. Grunwald. He had told me the story of being sold as an eight-year-old slave and showed me his scarred back on the day he taught me to shoot, but after that, he never spoke of his past again.

Mr. Grunwald stood in the buggy and gazed back toward the house a couple hundred yards away. He smiled as he looked to Curley. "How long has it been since you've been to town?"

Curley shrugged.

"Well I think it's high time you went in to see what you are missing." He handed the reins down, then skipped to the ground on the other side of the buggy. "I ordered some things from Mr. Smithson last week. They ought to be in by today. Why don't you and Branson go on to town to get them for me?"

Curley swallowed and the expression on his face was..., fearful? "Mr. Grunwald, you know I can't do that."

"Nonsense, Curley. That was a long time ago and a long ways away. Nobody in Lawrence—."

"Please don't make me go." Curley paused, looking down at his boots. "Branson," he pointed to me, "he can get your things." He looked to Mr. Grunwald, the pleading evident in his eyes.

As I watched the exchange, I thought again of how much I didn't know about my best friend and hoped that someday he would tell me. I glanced at Mr. Grunwald and saw sadness there also.

"But Curley, I told you that President Lincoln has freed

the slaves. You don't need to be afraid to be seen in town."

Curley shook his head again. "I stay here."

Mr. Grunwald nodded. "Very well, Curley. Let's you and I walk back to the house. If you've left any peaches in the root cellar, maybe we can sit and you can tell me again that I'm the best farmer in all of Kansas."

The mood lightened and both men smiled. Curley handed me the reins, then stepped around the buggy to stand next to Mr. Grunwald. A silent moment passed between them before Mr. Grunwald nodded and reached to grasp Curley's shoulder. The respect each had for the other was obvious. I knew they had been together a long time and I longed for the day I'd know more.

What had happened in that long ago time and faraway place that made Curley afraid to go into town? I looked away, feeling somehow that my watching their moment of friendship was meddlesome. I climbed into the buggy and without a backwards glance, started toward town.

Saddled horses lined the spaces in front of the closest saloon on that hot, August afternoon. I drove by and even though they had nothing to do with me, I noticed there were ten. Four sorrels, five bays and a gray. I smiled to myself as I realized how much Curley's teaching had become such a part of me. I stopped the buggy at the store, tied the reins around the seat rail and skipped down to the dusty street. Unlike the saloon, the store was empty.

The door was propped open in the afternoon heat and I could see all the way through the store to the back door, which was also open for any air movement. As I stepped to the door, I felt the hot breeze as it blew through. Mr. Smithson ignored me for a moment as he stealthily stalked a fly on the counter. With practiced speed, he slapped with his worn and bent fly swatter, then scraped the dead fly to the floor. He turned to me with a smile while hanging the instrument of death on a nail. "Good afternoon, Branson.

Hot enough for you?"

I chuckled at the timeworn joke. Not because it was funny, but because it was expected. I leaned on a molasses barrel and rubbed the scarred wood of the counter. "Mr. Grunwald sent me to pick up some things he ordered last week."

"Of course. I've got it all over here." He pointed toward the back of the store, then, with a wave over his shoulder, he bade me follow.

He carried one box while I carried the other, noticing with no small amount of vanity that he had given me the heavier of the two. Curley had been doing the same as of late. I felt a surge of pride that they no longer treated me as a boy, but as a man. We loaded the boxes into the buggy, then both stepped onto the boardwalk in the shade. He leaned on a post and turned to see the street. I tucked my thumbs into my pockets and followed his gaze.

Three men rode from east to west on the busy street. I normally wouldn't have paid much attention at the common sight, but I leaned forward with wide eyes. I could scarcely believe it, but the paint horse one of the men rode was the horse I'd seen leading Old Jackson away from the barn on that terrible day. For a moment, I was eleven again, and I felt the rage and fear I'd felt that day.

I turned abruptly and walked under the shade to keep pace with the riders. Curley had mentioned something about only three men left in the outlaw group. I had every reason to believe these might be the men who'd killed my family, but I was alone and there were three of them.

The boardwalk ended and I stepped to the dirt next to the blacksmith shop. I paused at the hitching rail as they turned their horses and pulled to a stop. They dismounted and were only feet from me. I gripped the smooth, worn wood of the hitching rail while studying their faces, one at a time. A sudden doubt surfaced. They seemed to be ordinary men and I couldn't see the expected look of evil in their eyes. For these years, I had held the image of the men I'd someday kill, and that image didn't meld with the men who returned my gaze. I tried to see their hands, for if any was missing a finger, that would be evidence enough for me, but each of the men wore gloves.

"Howdy, young feller." One spoke and two nodded pleasantly before walking through the open doors of the smithy's shop.

I didn't speak. I couldn't. I had waited with guarded anticipation for the moment I looked into the eyes of the men who'd killed my family, but that wasn't the moment. I studied the paint horse again. It certainly looked the same, but that had been a long time ago and I hadn't been all that close back then. I frowned in disappointment. How many paint horses were there in the state of Kansas? I took off my hat and wiped the sweat from my brow, then looked again to the men who now stood inside talking with the smithy. I shook my head and stepped to the boardwalk, using the post to pull myself up. My constant thought had been revenge, but a seed of doubt grew in my chest. What if I never found them?

Mr. Smithson continued his leaning against the same post when I returned. Sweat dripped from his chin and he fanned himself with a thick sheet of paper.

He stood as I approached and motioned down the street with his nose. "Why all the interest in the Tulare brothers?"

My head snapped up. "You know them?"

He shrugged. "Some. They come in on occasion."

"Do they live around here?"

"Sure do." He stood from the post. "I figured you'd know who they were."

"Why's that?"

He swallowed and hesitated. "Well, 'cause they live on your old homestead."

I turned quickly to look down the boardwalk toward the blacksmith shop. "Our old place?"

"Yep. For a year or more."

I had only been to my old home one time since that day, and that was to get the few things out of the barn that Curley and I could salvage. I felt a sudden regret that I hadn't visited the grave. It may have been cold-hearted of me, but I preferred to remember Ma alive rather than dead. I looked back to Mr. Smithson as I thought about the Tulare brothers. They lived at our place and one rode a paint horse. Was it a simple coincidence? A drop of sweat rolled down my back causing an involuntary shudder. I needed to talk to Curley. He would know what to do.

Randall Dale

Chapter 9

The mare pushed her nose out, raised her tail and trotted all the way home with a rhythmic clickity-clop rising from the hard-packed road. I drove straight to the barn in the dwindling light. When I pulled her to a stop, I stood in the buggy and called for Curley.

He wasn't at the barn so I skipped to the ground and ran to his cabin. "Curley? Curley, where are you?"

No answer came. I looked around, then at seeing nothing, returned to the buggy. After taking care of the mare, I pushed the buggy to the place Mr. Grunwald always left it, then in two trips, carried the boxes from Mr. Smithson's to the covered porch next to the back door.

By that time the light of day had slowly pulled away leaving only the lingering dusk. I didn't know where Curley had gone, but lanterns burned in the house.

I stamped my feet to knock the dust from my boots, then strolled into the house and hung my hat on one of the pegs by the door. I smelled the heavenly scent of Mrs. Grunwald's delicious chicken and dumplings stew. It drew me like a magnet to the dining room where I heard voices in pleasant conversation. When I entered, Mr. and Mrs. Grunwald sat at either end of the long table, and to my surprise, Curley, with a pleasant expression, sat on the side between the two. His bowl, scraped clean from what I could see, was pushed away and he held the cloth napkin in his folded hands as they rested on the table.

Mr. Grunwald looked up. "Splendid, splendid, my boy. Take a seat and eat."

Mrs. Grunwald jumped to her feet. "Hello, Branson." She left without waiting for an answer and returned from the kitchen with another plate and spoon. She slid them to the place opposite Curley, but I didn't move. This had certainly been a day of firsts. It had started when Mr. Grunwald and Curley had expressed appreciation for one another in open and honest terms, and now Curley was eating a meal in their house.

I smiled. "Hello, Curley. Good to see you here."

He fingered the napkin and nodded pleasantly. "Branson." He leaned forward, reaching one of his huge hands across the table to push the dish of stew toward me.

I emptied the large ladle into my bowl, winked at Mrs. Grunwald and started on the delicious meal. I was anxious to talk to Curley, but I was a growing boy and needed my strength.

They discontinued the conversation they had been having and all was quiet as they watched me eat. I didn't know what they'd been talking about, but wished they would continue because I felt uncomfortable at their staring.

I stopped at only one bowl, pushing back and folding my arms. "Thank you, Mrs. Grunwald. That was delicious."

"Wouldn't you like more?"

I would have liked more, another three bowls or so, but I had pressing business to attend to. "No thank you, ma'am."

She shook her head and rose to begin clearing the table.

Curley and I helped while Mr. Grunwald smoked a cigar with arms folded and legs crossed.

When the dishes were washed, dried and put away, Curley nodded to the lady of the house. "Thank you, ma'am. I believe that was the most pleasant meal I has ever eaten."

She beamed with pride and touched him caringly on his cheek. I watched with amazement. I'd seen more feelings between the Grunwalds and Curley that day than I had the entire time I'd lived in that house. It was as though they knew their time together was short, but, looking back, I'm certain they had no idea how short that time was to be.

My impatience grew. I wanted to take Curley by the arm and drag him outside so I could tell him about the horse and the Tulare brothers, but he lingered, looking at the couple for a full minute before turning to me.

"Did you bring the goods from the store?"

"I did. Two boxes on the porch."

"And you took care of the mare and the buggy?"

I nodded.

He touched my shoulder. "You be a good boy, Branson Hawk." He turned to the couple. "Thank you again for the meal and for all you done for me. Good night."

"Good night." They answered in unison.

I followed Curley down the hall to the back door. He opened it, then turned and stood in the doorway. "Good night, Branson."

I looked at him in the dim light from the kitchen lantern. His dark face showed the hint of a smile.

He motioned toward the kitchen with his head. "They be good folks." He stepped over the threshold and out the door.

"Curley?"

He turned. "Yes."

"I saw one of the horses the marauders rode when they killed my family."

His head jerked up. "Today?"

"Yes, in town."

"Are you sure?"

I grunted. "Mostly. I was at the store when they rode by, three of them. Didn't you tell me that there were three left of the gang that raided our place?"

He scowled. "Yes. That be what I heard."

I stepped out the door and pointed east. "They are living on our place."

His eyes opened wide. "You mean the Tulare brothers?"

I frowned. "You know them?"

"Know of them. I hear they come from down south a ways."

"I wouldn't know about that, but if it's them, I've waited a long time for this. Let's go."

He held his hands up, palms out. "Whoa! Slow down a bit there. It might not be the same horse. After all, it's been more'n two years. Remember what I said. Slow and steady. Always slow and steady."

I put my hands on my hips in sudden anger. "Seems like slow and steady means doing nothing at all?" My tone had a bite and as soon as the words were out of my mouth, I regretted them.

He folded his arms and cocked his head. He didn't seem angry, and for that I was thankful.

"I'm sorry, Curley. I shouldn't have said that."

"No, you are right that we need to do something. What I meant was, let's don't do anything foolish until we know for sure these three were the marauders. You be fine with that?"

I took a deep breath. He was right, as always. Rushing in and gunning down three men simply because one of them rode a horse that looked like one I'd seen would not be wise. "How can we find out if they were the ones?"

"How about we go over there tomorrow and ask 'em?"

I frowned. "Just like that? Go knock on the door and ask them if they killed my family? If they are the ones, they'll kill us without thinking twice."

He shook his head. "It only takes one to answer the question. We can wait until we have a chance to talk to one without the others around."

I gazed into the moonlight toward our old homestead. "Tomorrow?"

"Yes, tomorrow."

Early the next morning we saddled two of Mr. Grunwald's riding horses and started east. I held my rifle in the crook of my arm. It was charged and ready. Curley's rifle was tucked into a scabbard under his right stirrup. The big man looked at me as we trotted along, the lines on his face set hard at the task ahead. In my nervousness, my breathing was shallow. I had imagined this moment for a long time, but now that it had arrived, I wondered if I was ready.

We circled to the high ground above the cabin and waited there, looking down in the morning light. The fields I'd plowed as a boy were green with tall corn plants. They looked far better than any crop I could remember from my youth. A cabin, an actual cabin and not a make-do dugout, stood not far from where our barn had been, and a new, tall barn with sturdy, attached corrals had been built nearby.

The minutes stretched past us one by one as we waited for, but never saw any sign of movement. Curley shifted the rifle he had taken from the scabbard to his other arm and leaned on the saddle horn.

"Don't appear to anybody home."

"Seems that way." I pointed to the barn and corrals. "Reckon we could slip on down and see if their horses are there?"

He sat straight in the saddle and placed a percussion cap to his rifle, I did the same. When finished, he pushed his rifle forward as a signal. I nodded, then kicked my horse ahead, leading the way with Curley following. When we got to the back of the barn, I stood in my stirrups to look through the slits. Several draft horses stood in their stalls with heads down and tails swishing at flies, but there was no sign of riding horses in general or of the paint horse in particular. I turned and whispered to Curley, "No riding horses inside. The brothers must be gone."

He relaxed in the saddle and I turned my horse toward him. He frowned slightly and cocked his head. "Then I suppose we be done here. At least 'til tomorrow."

We rode side-by-side in solemn silence toward the Grunwald's, both lost in our own thoughts. As for me, the thought of revenge was strong. It grew closer day by day and I could feel it in my shoulders. I'd waited years for action, and was happy to finally be doing something. Curley's slow and steady pace had been fine for teaching, but action was now called for. We had been unsuccessful that day, but the time was short until we would find one of the men alone. We would make the trip every day if necessary.

My imagination ran wild during the mindless ride through the open prairie. I saw the men one by one as they looked with fear into my eyes and knew the reason I'd hunted them down. One by one, I bested them. There was no room in my heart for mercy, for they'd shown my family none. When the time came, I'd pay them back in kind.

So engrossed was I in my daydreaming that I didn't notice Curley sit straighter in his saddle until he reached and touched my arm. I pulled my reins. "What's wrong?"

He squinted, searching into the distance.

Several miles away a wispy, white cloud of smoke grew suddenly thicker and darker as it rose to the sky, and it was coming from the direction of the Grunwald's! In an instant both horses charged ahead, sprinting toward home with Curley and I leaning forward on our mounts, spurring them to increasing speed. The miles passed under us with unbearable slowness, and with each lunge of the horses, the smoke grew darker and more menacing.

When the house came into view, flames leaped from the roof, dancing high into the air and disappearing into the dense smoke. Behind the house, the barn was also engulfed in flames as was Curley's cabin, and as we approached, I saw that even the root cellar had fire leaping through the wide open door. There was no doubt that the fire had been set on purpose.

"Mr. Grunwald? Mr. Grunwald?" Curley frantically screamed toward the house. No answer came.

We advanced as much as possible, but the heat was unbearable so we rode in a hurried circle around the burning homestead with our arms held over our faces. We saw no sign of the couple, but we did see where the livestock from the barn had had been driven in a southeasterly direction. It didn't take much imagination for me to guess their destination, for we'd come from there only an hour before. We moved away from the heat and pulled our horses to a stop. They stood breathing heavily with legs braced wide and heads down. They had given more than we had a right to expect and were all done in.

Curley's head jerked suddenly, looking toward an old, abandoned hand-dug well away from the house. The only thing that remained of the original structure were the crumbling walls, and as I followed Curley's gaze, I saw the figure of a man leaning there. We jumped from our horses and sprinted to his side.

Mr. Grunwald gripped an old Colt Root pistol in his fingers as he leaned against the wall of the well with head lolled to the side and at least three bullet holes in his chest. To my surprise, he opened his eyes when we approached.

Curley knelt and held the man's shoulders. "Mr. Grunwald?"

A labored breath escaped and with help, Mr. Grunwald straightened his head. "Hello, Curley." The voice was ragged, rasping, and when he coughed, blood flecked the corners of his mouth.

"The Missus? Where be the Missus?"

A weak shake of the head. "In the house. Dead."

Curley wilted and I thought he might fall to the dirt. Instead, he reached and tenderly opened Mr. Grunwald's shirt exposing three puckered holes. Dark, purple blood oozed from each. Curley leaned him forward and pulled the shirt from his shoulders. Three jagged exit wounds were not so sparing with the bleeding and a pool of blood had gathered at the base of the wall where Mr. Grunwald sat. I didn't know how he was still alive.

Curley let him lean again on the wall of the well. "Who done this."

Mr. Grunwald coughed again and blood dripped from his lips. "Three raiders. Didn't get a good look." A wave of pain caused his face to contort and his whole body to stiffen, then, as death claimed the body, all the muscles relaxed and he slowly slipped to the dirt.

Curley wailed and buried his face in his hands. His shoulders shook and his breath caught in his throat.

My shoulders dropped at the loss of my second family, and as I studied Curley, I realized that the Grunwalds had been his second family also.

After a time, he turned to me and the fire in his eyes seemed to match the intensity of the fires raging in the house and barn. "Let's go." He hurried to his horse, gathered the reins and gripped the saddle horn.

I hustled to catch up. "Go where?"

His eyes squinted as he motioned with his head. "Back to your old place. There be some men there that need killin'."

I shook my head at the reversal of our roles. I could scarcely believe that I was the one holding back. "No, Curley. The horses are plumb give out. Besides, if we go now, we will come up on their cabin in broad daylight. They'd pick us off like turtles on a fence before we could get close enough to tangle with them."

He swallowed hard and dropped his head.

I stepped closer. "We didn't pass them on the way so they must have gone somewhere else. If there was ever a time for slow and steady, this is it."

His nostrils flared as he took a deep breath, then, without warning, he reached to pull me close and rest his forehead on my shoulder. His chest heaved and his breath jerked in and out as a second wave of grief overtook him. I held him like he'd held me three years earlier. I had needed comfort from him then, and now the tables were turned. No words were spoken, only an honest embrace with no thought as to the differences of our skin or our age.

We stood in the grip for a full minute until he straightened and took a step back, then gazed at me with a mournful expression. "They was like family to me. Long years ago they done took me in and hid me from the slave catchers. They took a terrible chance. I owe them my life."

I watched in fascination as the expression on his face turned from soulful to determined. He nodded and turned to strip the saddle from his mount. I followed his lead, then we led them to a natural pond not far from the house for a well-deserved drink. They drank their fill, splashing with their noses at the water and pawing into the mud. We led them to some tall prairie grass and tied hobbles to allow them to graze the night through.

We walked with heavy steps and heavier hearts back to the abandoned well. Curley looked over the crumbling wall so I stepped closer and did the same. The well had caved in but was four feet deeper than the surrounding ground. Curley reached for the pistol, uncurling stiffening fingers until it came free. He turned it over and looked at it, then stuffed it into the front of his pants. With me at the feet and Curley at the head, we lifted Mr. Grunwald over the wall and let him slip into the depression, then pushed the wall over him. I turned to see the house and barn. The fires had weakened, but the smoke, seemingly thicker and blacker than before, continued to rise into the afternoon sky.

We made plans that night before sleeping next to our saddles. I suggested an ambush, shooting the men as they left the cabin. We each had a rifle and could kill two of the men with the first volley. I thought it a good plan, but Curley frowned.

"I been thinking about that and I'll admit that I was ready to go there and kill them for what they done." He reached and touched my arm. "Thank you for stopping me." He leaned back. "But the more I think about it, the more I know that we need to be smart. Is there a chance the brothers are not the marauders?"

I waved my arm at the burned buildings. "Somebody hit here this morning." I touched my finger. "And the Tulares were gone from their cabin this morning." I touched another finger. "One rides the same paint horse that I had seen when they killed my family." I held my hand up and gripped still another finger. "And they've taken over our homestead."

Curley exhaled. "Proof enough to kill them?"

As much as I wanted revenge, I concluded that he had a point. He'd constantly drilled into me that jumping into things without thinking was unwise. I had tried to learn, but that approach went against my nature. I took a breath and exhaled. "What do you suggest?"

"Same plan as today. Get one of them off by hisself."

The next morning, long before daylight, we removed the hobbles from the horses, watered them again and saddled for the long ride. They had grazed and we had eaten green corn on the cob from the lush fields. We picked more for our breakfast and ate as we trotted to our destination.

We arrived at the knob before the first glimmer of the sun came over the prairie to the east, happy to see the paint and two other horses in the corral. We rode to the back of the barn where we could not be seen from the cabin. I looked at Curley and he looked at me. It was payback time. We got off and climbed through the rails and into the front door of the barn.

Our wait was short as one of the men, leaving the cabin while pulling his suspenders over his shoulders, came to the barn. He walked past our hiding places, climbed the ladder to the loft and forked prairie hay to the draft horses in their stalls on the inside and to the saddle horses on the outside. When he climbed down the ladder, we met him at the bottom with both rifles pointed at his back. He froze when he felt the muzzles against his shirt and heard the unmistakable sound of hammers being drawn back on cap and ball rifles. He slowly raised his hands and I noticed with disappointment that he had all the fingers on both hands.

"That's bein' smart, young feller." Curley moved to the side so the man could see his face. "Where were you yesterday?"

The brother looked over his shoulder to see me, then turned his head again to Curley. "We went to town."

"Stop anyplace along the way?"

"No. Hurried right back here when we saw what the raiders had done."

Curley cocked his head. "We're of a mind that you be a raider?"

The Tulare brother smirked and turned to face his accuser. He looked at me again and bravely lowered his arms.

I pushed my rifle into his side. "Keep 'em up."

He frowned and looked me up and down, then raised his arms again. "We're jus' trying to make a living on this little homestead. It's hard enough without having to worry about that Quantrill feller."

My brows pulled low. What did Quantrill have to do with anything? The last we had heard he'd gone back to Missouri.

Curley also had a confused look on his face. "Quantrill?"

"Him and his gang raided Lawrence yesterday. Shot folks, burned buildings and stole what they could before running away like cowards. When we rode into town and found out, we skedaddled back here in case they came our way."

Curley took a deep breath and momentarily looked at me. His eyes squinted and he frowned as he tried to understand what the man had said.

I shook my head, also trying to think. If the man had told the truth, they weren't the raiders. I remembered their faces as they entered the blacksmith shop two days earlier. They didn't have the expressions I would have expected from marauders, but, I reasoned, how would I know what a raider might look like.

Curley pushed the rifle deeper into the man's back. "One more question. Where'd you get the paint horse in the corral?"

"Bought him from a man down at Spring Hill. That's where we come from before we moved here."

"Do you know the man's name?"

The brother studied the ground for a moment, then shook his head. "Can't recall the name. He showed up thereabouts close to the same time we come up here. About all I know is that he married the widow Farraday."

Curley lowered his rifle, but I wasn't quite ready to trust the man. What if he had lied? It would be easy to make up a story. I looked at Curley, then spoke. "Are either of your brothers missing a finger?"

The man frowned. "Nope. All of us have all ten." With his hands up, he wiggled his fingers so I could see.

Curley slowly nodded and motioned for me to back away. I took a deep breath of disgust, then moved to the door.

"Sorry to bother you. We needed to find out and now we know more." Curley placed his rifle in the crook of his arm and hurried to me.

We slipped through the rails and mounted, turning our horses away and leaving at a high lope. No sense in giving the Tulares anything to shoot at in case they thought we had overstepped our bounds. We pulled up a half-mile away.

"So, what now?"

Curley rubbed his beard. "The first thing we be wanting to do is go to Lawrence and see what the raiders did, then we go to Spring Hill to find the man who sold the horse."

I looked at my friend. The preparation and teaching had been for me to learn so I could go after the raiders, but plans had changed. Curley, unless I read him wrong, had joined me, and now the chase was as much his as it was mine. His reason, to punish the marauders for the death of the Grunwalds, and my revenge was for my family.

I changed the heavy rifle from one arm to the other, wishing I had a saddle scabbard like Curley. "You're coming then?"

He squinted his eyes and glared at me without speaking. After a moment, he kicked his horse into a steady trot toward town.

Chapter 10

The town of Lawrence on the wide, Kansas plain lay bruised and broken on that hot August day. Stores, which only days earlier had been busy with customers, were now blackened holes after being burned and looted. Only a few people with darting eyes braved the normally busy street. They rushed from one side to the other, ducking under the collapsed awning because the posts had been jerked free causing the overhang, if it hadn't burned, to sag, or in some locations, fall completely from the buildings. We rode down the street, heads turning from side to side to see the unbelievable damage. When we passed Mr. Smithson's store, I reined my horse to the boardwalk and stepped down. Curley followed my lead. We stood, leaning under the overhang to peer in. Mr. Smithson, with a bloody bandage around his head, sat on a blackened stool with his head in his hands. He glanced up, nodding.

I stepped to the boardwalk, ducking under the low-hanging roof. Before I entered I noticed that Curley continued to stand in the street. He'd removed his hat and held it nervously in his hands. I motioned inside. "Come on."

He shook his head. "I be staying right here,"

I was too naïve at the time to understand the reason for his reluctance. It wasn't until later, that I began to see.

I shrugged and entered alone. "Hello, Mr. Smithson."

He looked at me with blank eyes. In a moment he leaned back on his stool and waved his arm around the room. "Everything's gone."

My frown deepened. I felt sorry for the man. "Quantrill?"

He stomped his foot and swore. "No good Reb. He's not man enough to join the real fighting, but he's a mighty brave man when it comes to looting a defenseless town."

"Why Lawrence?"

"I hear tell it was because of the Red Legs."

"Red Legs?"

He cocked his head and looked at me. "You don't know about the Red Legs?"

I shook my head.

His shoulders slumped. "No, I guess you wouldn't. But you know that Lawrence was sacked once before the war?"

I remembered hearing about it. A gang of pro-slavery men led by, of all people, the county sheriff, ransacked the town because Lawrence was an anti-slavery stronghold. "Yes, I heard about it."

"Well, in retaliation, the Red Legs, made up mostly of Lawrence citizens, banded together to punish anyone who gave aid to pro-slavery raiders. They've been busy the last couple of years, rounding up and imprisoning mostly women and girls who had, or had been accused of helping any of the raiders. In truth, it was no surprise that Quantrill came to punish the town for what the Red Legs did."

I grunted. "How many raiders were there?"

He exhaled loudly and waved his arms with excitement. "Hundreds. They were everywhere. They come in at daybreak, shooting up the town and killing innocent folks. I hear the dead count is over a hundred and only a very few buildings escaped their wrath." He stood from his stool and looked about the room. "My whole life's work was wrapped up in this store, and now it's gone."

I sighed, saddened at what had happened to the town, and to Curley and me. "Will you be able to rebuild?"

His lips pressed together and he breathed deeply. "I don't know how I can. I have no money." He looked up hopefully. "Maybe the Grunwalds?"

I glanced out the door to see Curley standing with a frown. I looked back to Mr. Smithson while slowly shaking my head. "The raiders sacked their place too. Killed Mr. and Mrs. Grunwald and burned every building."

"No!"

"Afraid so." I nodded toward Curley. "Me and Curley are heading down to Spring Hill to find out who did it." I frowned. "We were thinking it was the same outlaws who killed my family, but if Quantrill was here yesterday, it could have been some of his men."

Smithson rubbed under the bloody bandage, then brought his hand away and looked at his fingers before turning to me again. "Could be. Like I said, there were hundreds of them."

I glanced to Curley and saw the tight lips and hard eyes. Going after three or four men responsible for the deaths of my family was one thing, but going against hundreds of Quantrill's raiders was something else altogether.

I stepped back in preparation to leave. Smithson stood and wiped his blackened hands on his blackened pants, then reached for a shake.

I shifted my rifle to my left hand so I could grasp his. "Good luck, Mr. Smithson."

"Same to you, Branson."

We mounted our horses and rode south, following a road churned up by hundreds of raider horses from the day before. I told Curley in short, clipped tones what I'd learned. Our mood, bleak before our trip through Lawrence, was all the more hopeless now. How could we, only two of us, possibly take on a couple hundred or more raiders? I waited for Curley to speak, and I suppose he waited for me, and because neither of us was inclined to conversation, the ride was silent.

By dark we had traveled halfway to Spring Hill. We made a cold camp under a lone oak tree next to a slow-moving stream. We built no fire in case any lingering raiders saw the light and decided they wanted what we had. They wouldn't have gotten much except our horses, but the horses were our most necessary possessions.

We saddled before light and headed out, tired and hungry, but determined. The orange ball of sun rose on our left, bringing welcome light and unwelcome heat. The wide expanse of the prairie changed slowly as we rode along. Instead of the mostly flat plain, the countryside became rolling with groves of trees springing up more and more frequently until the woods, with tall, old growth trees, closed in around the road.

I looked at Curley and saw the exhaustion. With his haggard face, hollow cheeks and bloodshot eyes, he seemed to have aged in the last two days. The perpetual grin I'd grown so accustomed to had long since disappeared. He rode with enduring determination, but his strength was not what it had been. He allowed me to take the lead, meekly following with no complaint or suggestion.

The small town of Spring Hill, surrounded by dense, old-growth trees, was new to me. My entire life had been spent close to Lawrence, with nary a single trip to anywhere else. I turned to Curley as we rode down the town's single, hard-packed dirt street. "Ever been here before?"

I took his lack of an answer to be a no. We looked from side to side at the false-fronted buildings. Green, broad-leafed ivy climbed the rough-cut wood sides and I smelled the dankness in the air. As we passed the eatery and smelled the delicious aroma, my stomach growled. Neither of us had eaten since nibbling on the scarcely ripe corn at the Grunwald's the day before. Neither of us had so much as a penny in our pockets. I looked wistfully at the diner before turning my head away. We had rifles, but in a short discussion after leaving Lawrence, we had decided not to try to shoot any game in case some of Quantrill's men were hiding in the woods. Best if we got to Spring Hill without attracting any attention.

Curley pointed to the side and I looked to see a large, hand-painted sign above the door. SPRING HILL DRY GOODS AND MERCANTILE. We dismounted and I looped my reins over the rail. There was no boardwalk, only a sturdy set of wooden steps leading up to the front door. I motioned for Curley to go ahead, but he stood beside his horse and once again, removed his hat. I thought it odd behavior, but I shrugged and climbed heavily up the steps and through the open front door.

"Afternoon." A middle-aged man with longish hair and a scraggly, tobacco-stained beard stood from behind the counter while wiping his hands on a stained apron. "Help you with something?" He glared at me while keeping a wary eye on my rifle.

I approached the counter with a quick look around the store. Other than the man, two ladies stood together at the back looking at some fabric. Neither seemed to notice me. I lowered the butt of my long gun to the floor and held the barrel with both hands. The man's expression grew less nervous.

"I'm looking for someone."

He retook his seat on the stool and folded his arms. His only answer was a nod, and though he may have been reassured that my rifle was not held at the ready, he didn't seem overly anxious to help a stranger.

I smiled, trying to put him at ease, but it was apparent that coming straight out and asking about the widow Farraday would get me no answers. I had a sudden thought. "Do you remember the Tulare brothers?" It was a gamble and I knew it, but one I had to take. The brothers had come to Lawrence and by all appearances seemed honest and hard-working, but what they'd been in Spring Hill was not known to me. I saw in an instant that my gamble was a good one.

He stood quickly with a grin. "The Tulares? Fine boys. Where they be now?"

I motioned north. "Up in Lawrence. Doing good. They sent us down here looking for the widow Farraday and her new husband."

"Yes, yes. As I recall, one of 'em did cotton to her a might a few years back. Fact is I think he was plumb upset that she chose Jacob over him." He smiled broadly. "Keep headin' south for a hundred yards. On the left you'll see a little white house under a tall tree."

He hurried around the counter to step out the door with me following. He stopped short when he saw Curley. The guarded expression returned and his eyes narrowed as he turned to me. He pointed his finger at my chest. "You git out of town!"

It took a moment for me to realize what he meant. I quickly shook my head. "He's a free man."

The storekeep swallowed hard. "You ain't a slave catcher?"

The question disgusted me. "Absolutely not!"

He nodded. "Then take some advice. You be only ten miles from Missouri and these woods be full of slave catchers. Them folks is liable to get riled right quick if'n they see him. You be careful or they'll take him and he won't be a free man."

My heart caught in my throat as I recalled Curley's

scarred back. The thought of anyone treating him that way again boiled a fury in me I'd hadn't felt since the day Ma was killed. Of a sudden, I craved a fight, the sooner the better. Then something that Mr. Grunwald had said rang in my ears. He had told Curley that the slaves had been freed by Lincoln.

I pursed my lips. "I thought the slaves had been turned loose."

The man looked at me like the naïve kid I was, and at his stare, I cursed my ignorance. Mr. and Mrs. Grunwald had been fine folks, had taken me in and cared for me, but they had not talked of politics so my knowledge was next to none.

The storeman pointed north and east. "Washington be a far piece from Eastern Kansas. The slaves was set free in any state in rebellion. Missouri ain't in the Confederacy so those slaves weren't set free."

I frowned. "But Kansas is a free state. How can there be slave catchers here?"

His eyes hardened and I could see the disgust in his expression. "Because they can be here tracking down escaped slaves and have them back in Missouri before anyone can do anything. The poor men get only a few hours of so called freedom, then they are gathered up and hauled back in chains." He slapped the counter in anger.

My shoulders dropped at the thought and I remembered the wagonfull of chained slaves I'd seen when I was younger. I nodded a solemn thanks, then lumbered down the steps and over to my horse. I looked back to the storekeep as he stood in the doorway. "Much obliged." I mounted.

Curley kept his head down, put on his hat and stepped on his horse. Together we turned and rode half of the hundred yards. I pulled to a stop and looked at him.

"Why are you acting this way?"

He studied the saddlehorn with a frown. At length, he turned in the saddle. "You has been a friend to me since we first met, but you don't know nothin' about how black folks is treated. Even here in Kansas where no slave is held, folks don't cotton to someone like me looking them in the eye."

I took a deep breath. There was so much I didn't know. I had grown, but I had no idea how the world worked. I nudged my horse down the street and stopped at the house under the tree. I stepped to the ground, then held the rifle in two hands. Curley slipped his from the scabbard and stepped off also. As I looked into his face, I was happy to see his determination had returned. With a nod to each other, we moved.

The hinges of the picket fence gate squeaked as I pushed it open. I marveled at the pleasant setting. Bright purple flowers lined the shaded walkway and the house had been recently whitewashed. A green-painted screen door and the open front door gave the impression of coolness with air movement through the shaded house. I glanced at Curley, then knocked loudly.

A girl came to the door holding a baby. She didn't speak for a time, but waited, I suppose for me to say my piece. I hesitated because from what I could see through the screen, she looked to be only slightly older than me. When the Tulare brother had mentioned the widow Farraday, my picture was of a much older woman. If this was the wife of the marauder who had killed my family, she was fixing to be a widow again.

I touched the brim of my hat trying to appear as though I posed no threat. Remembering the name the storekeep had given, I leaned to the screen. "Afternoon, ma'am. We're looking for Jacob. We hear tell he lives here."

She made no move to open the door, but she stepped closer and I could see what I took for fear in her eyes. She bent to set the baby on the floor and when she stood to face me again, I looked into the business end of a double-barreled shotgun. The fear I thought I'd seen was replaced with anger and mistrust.

"Who wants to know?"

I dared not tell the truth about our business, that would get me shot for sure. I'd come to the door with my rifle pointing down, and at that moment I lowered it further so as to be even less threatening.

"Only need to ask him a couple of questions." I remembered my approach with the store man. "Truth is we were sent here by the Tulare brothers. One of them mentioned you and we determined to set out this way to make your acquaintance."

"Issat right?" Her tone was biting. With hard-set eyes she pushed the scattergun toward us. "I'm thinking you should jus' back right on down the walkway and mount up and move on."

Her attitude riled me. "Ma'am, you got no call to treat us so. We came polite like. All we wanted to do was ask Jacob a question."

The barrels of the gun touched the screen and in doing so, they each looked like they were wide as saucers. Her voice hissed. "Polite like? You come to my door, both of you carrying rifles. What am I supposed to think? With all the fighting and raiding going on, no man or woman is safe no matter what side they think is right. Now, git afore I let loose both barrels of this here gut buster!"

I knew she meant it so I slowly backed away. When I got to the gate, I saw that Curley was already mounted and riding back the way we'd come.

I stepped into the saddle and trotted to catch up. When I did, he pulled to a stop. The saddle creaked as he turned toward me. He didn't speak, but waited for me. He had seemed to want me to take the lead, but suddenly I wasn't so sure. Was he testing me?

I pointed toward the house with my rifle. "You heard it all?"

He glanced at my pointing. "Yes."

"Did I do something wrong?"

"Not wrong. But think for a bit. You are asking after her husband so you can kill him. You can hardly blame her for running us off."

I frowned as I let out a breath. "Why didn't you stop me?"

He tilted his head and smiled. "Because you can't learn if you don't do things yourself." He took off his hat and wiped the sweatband, then dried his forehead with his sleeve.

I took a moment to watch two blackbirds flitting through the air, but I wasn't watching them as much as thinking about what he'd said. He was right. I couldn't learn if I relied on him to do all the thinking. I could see now that in his silence, he'd continued his teaching. I turned to face him. "What should I have done?"

"I'm thinking the best way to talk to him is to catch him unsuspecting same as we did at the Tulare's place."

Seeing his wisdom, I nodded. With a half-smile, I motioned forward with my head. "I think I know where he is."

"Where's that?"

I rested my rifle on the saddlehorn. "Did you notice the cooper's tools in the basket on the porch?"

He graced me with a thin smile and I chuckled at what I took to be an acknowledgement of the lessons I'd learned, particularly when it came to observation. He had taught me well.

I looked down the street. "When we rode into town I noticed the blacksmith shop had barrels outside. Reckon they make them there?"

"I imagine so."

We pushed our horses forward, riding toward the blacksmith shop. I glanced into the open-sided structure as we rode by, noticing two men working inside. We rode past to the end of the street then turned and made our way down an alley behind the buildings on the opposite side. We dismounted, holding our horses behind a tree. From where we stood, we had a clear view of the shop. If things proceeded as I predicted, we would know shortly if one of the men inside was Jacob.

We had waited only a moment when I nudged Curley. The woman, carrying the baby, walked swiftly along the street. A small boy, four or five, barefoot with patched overalls, ran to keep up with her. With furtive glances, she hurried inside the blacksmith shop to talk to the man in the back.

In a moment they came out. Jacob, I presumed, rubbed the woman's shoulder then gently pushed her back the way she'd come. She looked at him with wide, fear-filled eyes, then dropped her head and trudged toward home. The man, Jacob, looked up and down the street, then, with a shake of his head, returned to the shop.

I turned to Curley. "There's our man."

"Yep."

We kept a close eye on the goings on across the street. Both men worked steadily into the afternoon until the big man in the front took off his leather apron and hung it on a nail at the side of the shop. With a wave over his shoulder, he left the open-sided building and walked north.

I looked at Curley. He nodded slightly in signal that he was ready. Leaving our horses tied to the tree, we walked quickly across the street. We both held our rifles waist-high, fingers inside the trigger guards.

Jacob looked up from a half-finished barrel. He turned slowly with hands raised. His eyes showed fear, but he handled it well, I'll give him that. I searched his raised hands and saw ten, long, slender fingers. I motioned with my rifle for him to move away from the table. When he did, I stepped directly in front. I was surprised at his youth, for he seemed as his wife, to be not that much older than me.

He swallowed hard and licked his lips. "I've been

waiting."

"Maybe so, but not as long as I have." I resisted the temptation to pull my trigger. It would have been easy to do. It would take only a small tug. I clinched my teeth, forcing the words through. "You ever been to Lawrence?"

He blinked. "I don't know what you're talking about."

I placed the barrel of my rifle against his throat. "I think you do."

His eyes opened wide in terror. "All right. It was a mistake. I shouldn't have gone. I wish I'd never gone."

"Tell me about it."

He looked to the ground and took a deep breath. "They came riding in one day telling me how much fun it would be."

"Who?"

My cousin Wilbur and two of his friends. Me and Wilbur lived in Harrisonville at the time. They said they were riding into Kansas to do a little scouting. I was just a stupid kid looking for excitement. I didn't know they'd been running with Quantrill. They didn't tell me about that until we were on our way back." He shook his head. "I only went that one time and I'll regret it to my dying day."

My shoulders shook as in my imagination I saw them riding around our dugout, yelling, shooting and terrorizing my family inside. Without thought, my pressure on the trigger increased. "Today might be your dying day."

He shook his head. "Please don't hurt me. They made me take the mule."

"I don't care about the mule, what about my family?" I hissed the words while uncaringly forcing the barrel of my rifle deeper into this throat.

He coughed. "I caught the mule, that's all. I don't know anything else." He was close to tears, whether in regret or fear, I couldn't tell. Probably a combination of both.

I forced myself to take a deep breath. I could have killed

him there and then, but where would that have gotten me? He had been the man on the paint horse and not one of the men who'd shot Caleb or Ma, or one of the men who'd thrown the torches into the dugout taking the lives of the twins. I wanted those men and I wanted them bad. I took a half step back.

He bent over with one hand on a knee and the other at his throat. He took several breaths before he straightened and looked at me.

I studied him, trying to keep my reason. "One of them came away without a finger. Who was that?"

He nodded quickly, anxious to tell me what I wanted to know. "That was Cleatus. He said the woman done it."

"Did he tell you why?"

He shook his head. "Just that she attacked him and he had to push her to get away."

"And the woman?"

He shrugged. "Don't know anything. We lit out of there at a full run. I suppose them folks had to get them a new mule, but I'm sure they made out all right."

I glanced at Curley, wondering if Jacob was telling the truth. The old barn wasn't so far from our little dugout that he wouldn't have heard the shots. I rotated back to Jacob. "You didn't hear the shots?"

"I heard Wilbur shooting in the air, then someone with a rifle took a shot from a long ways away. After that we skedaddled out of there."

I could remember the paint and the other riders whipping Old Jackson to keep up. By all accounts, Jacob told the truth. "I want their names." I'd barely asked the question before he complied, spitting the words out as though they had a foul taste.

"Cleatus Frye, Rastus Frye and my cousin, Wilbur Cowan. They tried to get me to go out with them again, but I wouldn't."

Three names. I thought of the morning Curley had told me there were only three in the gang. That made sense now, Jacob had dropped out. "How long since you've seen any of them?"

His expression changed and he fidgeted. For the first time I saw in his eyes a hesitancy that hadn't been there earlier. He glanced from me to Curley and back. "A couple of years or more."

I could feel in my chest that it was a lie. I pushed the rifle back to his throat. "How long?"

"All right, all right. They came through here yesterday with several other men. Their horses were lathered and they looked like they had traveled a long way fast."

"Did you talk to them?"

"Not at length. They asked if I wanted to raid with them but I refused. They weren't too happy about that, told me I'd better watch my back. They turned their attention to my partner William, telling him to reset a shoe on one of their horses. While he did, I heard them talking among themselves of how they'd ransacked Lawrence with Quantrill. Then Cleatus bragged that he and Rastus and Wilbur had burned a farm outside of town."

Curley had been standing to the side, content to let me ask the questions, but he stepped forward in a rush. "Which side of town?"

Jacob shrank back at his intensity, shaking his head. "Didn't say. Only that they had a running fight with an old man."

"Where those three be now?" Curley stepped closer, his face and hate-filled eyes only inches from Jacob's.

The young man's fear of Curley must have been stronger than his fear of the marauders. He answered quickly. "I don't know about the others, but Wilbur lives in Harrisonville, across the line." He pointed east into Missouri.

"How far that be?"

"Thirty some odd miles."

Curley stepped back and looked at me. I could see in his eyes that he wanted to be away, riding toward Harrisonville, the sooner the better. I held up a hand for him to wait for a spell.

I turned to Jacob. "You were in the gang that killed my family."

"I didn't kill anyone." His voice was high-pitched, panicky.

"That may be true, but you admit you were there?"

His shoulder dropped, as did his head. "Yes."

"So I could pull this trigger now and send you to kingdom come. I've sworn that I'd do that very thing."

He shook his head as he looked at me. His eyes pleaded but he chose not to speak.

I glanced again at Curley. He watched me but made no move to tell me what to do. I could have killed Jacob. Fact was that had been my plan all along. But what would that have accomplished? I realized the answer in a moment of clarity. Nothing.

Chapter 11

The next stage of our journey was clear. We had to get to Harrisonville, but unless we got some nourishment soon, we would both be too weak to travel. I thought of the heavenly smell from the eatery we had passed, and of our empty pockets. I looked Jacob up and down. He didn't appear overly prosperous, but he undoubtedly had more than we did. And he had stolen my mule.

"Jacob, you admit to stealing our mule?"

He looked down. "I do."

"It's time you made payment, but from the looks of you, I'm guessing you can't pay what he was worth."

"I'll give you whatever you want. Just don't hurt me or my family."

"Right now Curley and I only need one thing." I gestured for Jacob to stand. "We're going to walk, friendly like, over to the eatery to get some food and you're going to pay. If you'll agree to that, we'll leave and you'll never see us again."

He rapidly nodded.

Curley refused to enter the eatery so Jacob and I went in. I got two plates heaping with fried beef in stew and a basket of biscuits. We leaned on the wall of an adjacent building ate our fill, then as we made ready to go, wrapped biscuits and several strips of fried beef into a cloth napkin. I tucked the bundle under my arm, and, after sending Curley to fetch our horses, turned to Jacob.

"You seem a smart man, Jacob. Go home to your family." I turned and hurried to the horses.

We rode at a fast clip out of town, past Jacob's house and into the thick woods beyond. The branches of the tall trees at the sides of the road grew together over our heads making a tunnel into which we rode. When we were well away, Curley pulled up so I did the same.

"We be heading toward Missouri?"

"Yes." I wondered at the question. He knew as well as I that Missouri was our destination. "So?"

He didn't answer, but got down and untied his scabbard and handed it to me over his horse's back, rifle and all.

"What's this?"

He frowned. "Do you remember what the storekeep told you?"

I closed my eyes, trying to remember exactly what I'd been told. My eyes flashed open. "He said the runaway slave catchers are in these woods."

Curley nodded. "That's right."

"But you are a free man?"

"Not exactly."

My head snapped to him. "What?"

"I been free in Kansas because it be a free state. But Missouri ain't no free state."

I leaned forward. "I'll tell them you are a free man."

His voice dropped to a whisper. "A runaway slave won't never be free."

My head spun. All this time I thought he had been free. I didn't know how slavery laws worked and he'd told me he had tried to run when he was younger. The scars on his back were proof that he'd been caught at that early age. He hadn't talked of his life since then, but it never crossed my mind that he was a runaway and still officially belonged to his owner.

My mind raced. "We'll have to keep you from those men."

He nodded. "Only be one way to do that."

"What way is that?"

"I be your slave."

My face wrinkled in distaste. "What are you talking about? I'll never own a slave as long as I live."

The thin line of his lips slowly opened and the corners turned up ever so slightly. "I be glad to hear you say that." He pointed east. "But when we gets to Missouri, you make sure e'rbody be thinking you is my master."

As much as I disliked the idea, I could see his reasoning. I didn't know if it was as bad as the storekeep had said, that they would take Curley and make him a slave again, but it wasn't worth the risk. I grunted my agreement, took the rifle and scabbard and tied it under my stirrup then tucked the pistol into the back of my britches.

We headed south until we came to a fork in the road. Someone had carved HARRISONVILLE with an arrow on a plank and nailed it to a tree. Following the sign, we turned east.

To our relief, we saw no one on the road, and the farms we passed were far enough off the road that the people didn't see us. The terrain grew wetter with large and small streams and occasional ponds or lakes as we continued east. We stopped for the night at a thick grove of trees far away from the road we'd been on. We had seen no sign telling us of the border, but I knew the slave state of Missouri was near. We hobbled the horses and ate cold beef and hard biscuits before finding sleeping places for the night.

I slept little. Unlike the prairie animals from around

Lawrence, the forest animals moved and made noise throughout the night. I dreamed repeatedly and uncomfortably of Curley walking in chains behind a horse I rode with me jerking him along at every chance. When the welcome gray of dawn finally came, I felt more tired than before, but every bit as anxious to get to Harrisonville. As soon as it was light enough to travel, we saddled the horses, led them to a stream to drink, then mounted to continue our journey.

We had ridden only a short distance when ahead on the road, a man stood examining his horse's front leg. As we drew alongside, he dropped the foot, looked up and smiled easily. His thin, light colored beard and moustache framing his strikingly blue eyes.

"Howdy gents. I was heading to Spring Hill but my horse seems to be favoring his leg." He patted the horse's shoulder.

Curley removed his hat and looked down and away from the man. It was so foreign to me to see him act the part of the slave. I could see any conversation was to come from me and me alone. I leaned out to see the lame leg, then settled back into my saddle.

"Sorry to hear that. We are on our way to Harrisonville."

He smiled more broadly, showing even, white teeth. "How about that? That's where I'm from." He rubbed the horse's leg again. "I can see I won't make it to Spring Hill so I'm supposing I'll head back home. Mind if I ride along for as long as I can keep up?"

I looked to Curley but he gave no indication of approval or disapproval. I shrugged as I looked back to the man. "Fine by me."

He leaned to his horse to mount, then turned sharply to me. I blinked hard at the sight of the rifle pointing at my stomach.

His smile was evil and showed the contempt he held for me. I shared in that contempt. How could I have been so stupid? My mind raced for a way to get away, but as each possibility came, it vanished just as quickly because the outcome would have certainly ended in my, and possibly Curley's, death.

Curley's eyes grew wide as he looked down at the rifle. His breath escaped and his shoulders sagged, and the most painful for me was the look in his eyes, a look of disappointment that we'd allowed ourselves to be duped so easily. I blamed myself and my inexperience and I realized that no matter what I'd told myself, I still had a lot to learn.

My right hand held my rifle but there was no way I could get it into action fast enough to make a difference. I thought that he wanted to rob us, but we had nothing of value. I looped my reins over the horn and slowly raised my hands. "I ain't got so much as a penny to my name."

"I figured as much." He motioned toward Curley with his head. "But that there nigger's worth at least twenty dollars."

My heart raced. It was worse than I thought. "But he's a free man."

The man chuckled and motioned forward with his head. "Not once we get him over the line."

"We?"

He chuckled again. "Not you, kid."

It was then that I heard the rattling and creaking of a wagon. I turned and saw a buckboard pulled by two mules. As it approached, my stomach sickened when I saw four black men and a young boy chained in the bed.

"Whoa." The mules obediently stopped and dropped their heads while the driver reached and pulled a rifle from the seat. "Good work, Buck." He stepped from the wagon and stood at the front of my horse, pointing his gun at my chest. "Now, kid, you take that long rifle by the barrel and pass it down nice and easy."

There was nothing I could do other than comply. My best option was to go along and hope I'd live long enough to turn the tables. I took the barrel of my rifle in my left hand and passed it down.

He looked at it for a moment, then sneered at me. "Ain't seen one of these old-timers in quite some time." He motioned to Curley's rifle in the scabbard under my stirrup. "That one too."

I passed it down. He studied it briefly, then turned, and one at a time, placed the barrels between the spokes of the wheels and bent them useless. With a smirk, he tossed them into the brush at the side of the road.

I thought of the Colt Root tucked into the back of my pants. They obviously didn't know I had it, for it was covered by my loose-fitting vest. I leaned back in an effort to keep it unseen.

"Get off your horses."

I reluctantly did as I was told. What else could I do? As soon as Curley and I stood next to each other on the ground, the driver grabbed the reins and led the horses to the back of the wagon where he tied them. By that time, the first man stood close to me while the driver, after jerking something from the seat of the wagon, walked to stand next to Curley.

I couldn't see what the man held, but it brought a rage in Curley like I'd never seen. He bellowed like a bull and lashed out with unexpected suddenness. The driver dropped to the ground like a sack of potatoes, but the attack had been anticipated by the first outlaw. He drove the butt of his rifle into Curley's face. I heard the sickening thud and before I could move, my friend collapsed. I whirled with every intention of grabbing the outlaw, but he was too fast. I froze when I saw the barrel pointed at me.

"Don't try it, kid."

He had me dead to rights. One move from me and I'd have been a dead man. As it was, I was alive, and as long as I stayed that way, my hope of rescuing Curley stayed alive as well. If they were going to kill me, they likely would have done so by then, so I raised my hands and stood still.

The driver rolled to his side with a grunt and groan. He rested there for a full minute, then pushed to his knees and finally, somewhat unsteadily, to his feet. He reached to the dirt and lifted the chains and buckled them around Curley's ankles. My disgust was complete and I vowed to myself that I'd get Curley away if it was the last thing I did.

While the first man held his rifle on me, the driver walked to the wagon and unlocked the chain running through each of the slaves' ankle shackles.

"Get down and load him in the wagon."

Each of the men momentarily looked away, then in wearied, worried reluctance, each jumped to the ground. They hefted Curley's limp body into the wagon, then, because the shackles made it difficult, they helped each other until all were seated in the bed.

When the long chain was once again in place and none of the slaves, including Curley, could escape, the driver climbed the front wheel to the seat and slapped the reins on the mules' backs and headed east toward Missouri.

I watched in helpless resignation until the first man, who'd seemed so friendly an hour earlier, ordered me to sit on the dirt and take off my boots. I paused for a moment. I had the pistol but with his rifle constantly pointed at my chest, I would be a fool to go for it. I slowly unlaced my boots, took them off and set them at my side.

"Toss them over here."

I frowned. "Are you going to leave me stranded?"

He looked at me without sympathy. "I suppose I could kill you." He nodded toward the rifle he held, then squinted his eyes and grinned humorlessly.

As much as I hoped otherwise, I suspected he would not hesitate to do as he'd said. I flipped the heavy boots to him, biding my time until I could make a move, but he kept his distance and never wavered in his aim.

"Now, you jus' sit there and don't try to follow." He gathered his horse's reins as well as my boots and walked backwards down the road.

I slowly pulled the pistol from the small of my back, but fought the temptation to start shooting. In the first place, the old Root itself was not known as an accurate pistol, and second, I had not practiced with it a single time. I decided to wait until I had a close shot.

Thirty yards down the road, the slave catcher mounted and spurred into the distance. I jumped up and ran after him but knew I could never catch him. In dismay, I studied the tracks of his horse and the wagon. I didn't notice anything out of the ordinary in the horse tracks, but the right rear wheel of the wagon had a crack in the iron which made an identifiable track on the dusty road. My whole focus turned to following the tracks. I couldn't hope to catch up, but if the wagon ever left the road, I planned on finding Curley and getting him away from the slave catchers.

The sun rose higher in the sky and I began to question my ability to continue walking. My socks, now shredded, offered little protection for my feet, but I continued. I couldn't let the catchers get so far ahead that I would never find them. If I could find something to be thankful for that day, it was that the road held no rocks and was deep with powdery dust from the wagons and horses that passed there.

I kept a close watch forward and back. Three times I saw wagons on the road, but hid myself in the brush of the roadside as they passed. I was equally evasive if I saw a farm. I simply couldn't take a chance because I didn't know who I could trust. I'd already made one devastating mistake that day and I had no intention of repeating it.

Slightly after noon, a sign at the side of the road with MISSOURI carved deeply into the wood grain told me I was crossing the line, but there was nothing more than the marker to give any indication of the change. There was no difference in the countryside or the plants or trees, and the occasional farms looked the same. Yet, Missouri was a slave state and I trudged forward not knowing what to expect.

About two miles inside the line, I saw two log cabins and a set-back barn with planted fields on each side. To my surprise, the wagon tracks turned into the lane. I faded back into the trees and hid there while watching. I saw no one, which to me seemed unusual given the fields with tall corn pushing toward the sky. I would have expected some field hands taking care of the crop.

I backtracked to the edge of the westernmost field and entered, hiding in the rows of corn plants as I moved through. I found a hidden location close to one of the cabins and squatted on my haunches as I considered the buildings. Each seemed to be about twenty feet by twenty feet with only a door and no windows. I looked at the barn sat back from the cabins and wondered if the wagon, our horses and possibly my boots were inside.

I plucked two ears of corn and ate them while studying the layout. I saw a possibility, so I faded back into the field and made my way to the back side of the barn. I hesitated until I was mostly certain no one was there, then I hunkered down and hurried to the partially open door. Once inside, I stood by a post, hiding there in case I'd been mistaken. I breathed a sigh of relief when I saw the wagon, mules and our horses, but no person.

I shuffled over to the wagon and was ecstatic when I saw my boots haphazardly thrown into the bed. I plucked them out and sat on an old box to slip them on. My feet had swollen, but I forced the boots on, tied the laces and stood. For the first time since we'd been bushwacked, things were looking up.

Of a sudden, I heard dogs barking so I rushed from the barn and back into the field. To my great relief, the dogs weren't barking at me. Rather, they stood at the door of the cabin closest to the road and constantly yapped at an approaching buggy. I watched as the door to the cabin opened and the men who'd taken Curley stepped to the porch with waves of welcome.

The buggy pulled to a stop and the driver, a heavyset man in a business suit, stepped down. Each of the men walked to shake his hand, then the slave catcher Curley had knocked to the ground hurried to an adjacent cabin. From his pocket, he pulled a ring of keys and unlocked a padlock before swinging the door inward.

"Come on out."

One by one the four men and the boy I'd seen in the wagon, all with shackles around their ankles, walked into the light of day holding their hands over their eyes because of the bright, afternoon sun. I waited for Curly but he didn't come out. The catcher must have also been waiting because he hollered again.

"You come on out or I'll send the dogs in." He stepped back from the door.

Relief mixed with anger filled my breast when my friend, chains connecting his legs and arms to a metal clamp on his neck, shuffled out of the cabin. Unlike the others, he couldn't raise his hands against the sun because of the chains. He squinted and ducked his head, then stumbled and fell forward after being brutally pushed from behind by slave catcher.

The white man cursed, then viciously kicked Curley in the ribs. It took all my 'slow and steady' training not to run and put a bullet in the man. He deserved it and I was ready to deliver, and I would have if I'd held one of those new repeating rifles I'd heard about instead of the slow-to-fire cap and ball pistol shoved into the back of my pants. But as bad as my friend's situation was at the moment, it would be worse if I got myself killed before setting him free.

Curley rolled and clumsily pushed to his feet. I wished I

had some type of signal to give him hope, but that would have to wait. He joined the others standing in a line close to the buggy. All had heads down in terrified submission. I blinked when the newcomer examined each in turn and I realized that he was there to buy slaves.

I was too far to hear the men talking, but it was obvious they haggled over prices. When finished, they forced the boy into the back seat of the fringe-topped buggy, removed his leg irons and chained his hands to a side rail. I wasn't too far to see the horrified look on his face.

It appeared the business was completed until the new man stepped in front of Curley. He asked a question and I saw Curly submissively shake his head. The three white men had another conversation, then the catcher with the keys unlocked the neck clamp and tossed it to the side, then did the same with the leg and arm shackles. Curley climbed into the buggy and compliantly held his hands at the side rail so he could be chained in.

My mind raced. If Curley was leaving, I needed to be on the road. I turned and ran through the corn rows to the woods next to the lane. I examined my options. I could ambush the man. He was, after all, only one man and I had the pistol. I could easily free Curly. I looked back to the cabin and concluded that the ambush would have to be farther away lest the slave catchers came running if they heard a shot.

From my hiding spot, I saw from the tracks on the road that the buggy came from the Missouri side, which was no surprise. If I could get in front, I could make my move away from the clearing. I crossed the road and jogged ahead, then slowed to a steady walk, looking over my shoulder ever minute. Finally, the buggy pulled from the lane and the horse steadily clip-clopped toward me.

"Whoa." The buggy stopped next to me and the driver looked down. "Afternoon."

Curley didn't glance up and I ignored him, placing all my attention on the driver.

"Afternoon." My concern was that we were still too close to the slave catchers place, but, we were where we were and I had no choice but to make my play. I stepped closer and slowly reached for the handle of my pistol, but stopped at his words.

"Need a ride?"

I nodded and forced a smile. "If you've got room."

He pointed over his shoulder with his thumb. "You can sit in the back with the boy."

It was better than I'd hoped. We could get farther down the road and I would be in the back seat out of the man's sight. "Obliged."

I climbed in and sat heavily in the leather seat. Curley sat facing outward with his head down and made no move to indicate that he'd seen me, but I was sure he had. I studied his bruised face and the anger in me rose again.

A half-mile down the road I retrieved my pistol and placed it against the back of the driver's head. The click of the drawn hammer was loud and the man tensed in sudden recognition of what was happening.

"Stop the buggy."

He complied, pulling on the reins with measured slowness. When we stopped, I stepped to the dirt still holding the pistol against his head. He looked at me from the corner of his eye and I could see the terror there. Good, I thought, the more afraid you are the quicker you'll do everything you are told to do.

"Unlock the chains."

He hesitated for only long enough for me to push the pistol harder against his head. I was in no mood to be gentle. He swallowed hard, then, moving slowly so as not to get me trigger happy, he pulled a key from his vest pocket and reached over Curley's legs to release the chain around his hands and the rail.

Curley threw the chain to the dirt and jumped from the buggy. He turned and jerked the key from the driver's hand and unchained the boy, who also jumped to the ground. In his terror, he made ready to run, but Curley, anticipating the move, reached to grasp his thin arm.

"Hold on their, son. You head out now and another slave catcher will have you locked up 'fore morning. Stay with us. We'll get you to Kansas." He looked at me with a questioning glance.

I nodded my agreement. When we started our trip, our only goal was to find the murderers in Harrisonville, but they would have to wait. Seeing Curly in irons and sold like a horse made it so. Our quest for revenge could wait a few days, for there were men who needed our help, and we seemed to be the only ones willing to help them escape and get to Kansas. I pointed back the way we'd come. "And we'll get the others too."

The buggy creaked as the driver shifted in the seat to see me. He looked like he wanted to say something but quickly decided not to, I suppose because he saw the deadly look in my eye as my disposition at that time was far from cordial.

"Get down from the buggy."

He awkwardly stepped down, then raised his hands high over his head. What to do with him? I didn't want him following us because we needed to get back to rescue the poor devils locked in the dark cabin. I looked around, then had a thought. "Curley, pass me those irons. Let's see how he likes 'em."

The man whimpered and I thought he might cry, but I had no sympathy for a man who would own another. With my pistol, I motioned toward the woods at the side of the road. "Over there."

We walked several yards into the thick trees and brush, and with every step his protestations increased. "Don't chain me mister. I've never done anything to you."

I didn't answer other than to tell him to get on his hands and knees so I could put the irons on his ankles without him standing and possibly attacking me while I bent down.

He grew more agitated as he sank to the grass and weeds under the trees. "I can pay. Anything you want."

I pushed him forward until his hands were also on the grass, then with a loud click, buckled the shackles around his ankles. He descended to his belly to lay and cry, but I did not care. I had no need for his money and any sympathy I might have felt had long since departed. It didn't seem to bother him to chain another, but it was a different story when the unforgiving metal surrounded his ankles.

"You call out to the next wagon down the road. Maybe they'll help you and maybe they won't. Don't much matter to me one way or the other."

Without waiting for an answer, I turned back to the road. Curley and the boy were already seated and had turned the buggy to head back the way we'd come. I stepped in and patted Curley on his shoulder. He took a deep breath, then passed me a rifle.

I took it with a questioning glance. "Where'd this come from?"

Under the seat. It's one of them newfangled Henry repeating rifles. I'm a thinkin' that it'll be mighty handy when we go a calling on them there slave catchers."

I looked at the rifle, turning it over in my hands. It was considerably shorter than my old muzzleloader. I worked the action, ejecting a small cartridge only as big around as my pointing finger and not much more than an inch long. I held it in my fingers and studied it, intrigued that it held powder, ball and primer all in one. I'd heard Curley and Mr. Grunwald speaking of repeating rifles, but had never seen one. I glanced at the boy in the back, then nodded toward Curley. "Then let's go a calling."

He slapped the reins on the sorrel. "Giddap."

The afternoon sun touched the tops of the trees behind the cabins and barns. With strict instructions to the boy to stay with the buggy on the road, Curley and I peeked around the cornfields trying to decide the best approach. I put a hand on his shoulder. When he turned to me, I pushed the rifle toward him, but he shook his head.

"You be keeping that, young Branson Hawk. You're a man now. You deserve it. I knew you would come for me and come you did." He touched my shoulder. "You saved my life. Thank you."

I cocked my head. There were times I felt every bit of the man he described, then, as in thinking about being deceived that afternoon by the slave catchers, I felt inadequate. I reached to pull the Colt from my waistband. "Very well." I pushed the gun toward him. "Then you take this."

He took the pistol from my hand and checked the loads. Satisfied, he looked toward the cabin where the two men stayed. "They've got dogs."

I frowned as I turned my attention to the cabin, remembering the ruckus the dogs raised when the buyer drove into the yard. "Yes, they do. As soon as they see us, I suspect those mongrels will bark to high heaven and the catchers will come out loaded for bear."

As I stood, my legs began to quiver so I lowered to my knees to rest. I'd walked ten miles in my stocking feet and I was plumb give out. Curley joined me there and as we took the time to rest, we watched the cabin while trying to decide our best option.

I remembered the barn and the horses and mules there. I pointed with the rifle. "They've got to come out sooner or later to feed the livestock. Maybe if we go to the barn we can surprise them."

He touched the bruised and scraped side of his face. "I think I be liking that."

I led the way, circling across the road and into the cornfield on the other side. As we walked down the rows, we each picked ears of corn to devour for the strength we would need. We paused for a time at the edge of the field to make sure neither of the slave catchers had gone to the barn undetected. When satisfied, he motioned for me to go ahead so I hunkered down and ran to the partially open door. Lucky for us, the dogs, on the front side of the cabin, couldn't see me so I entered undetected. Once I was inside, Curley joined me.

An open stall gave me a good hiding spot. I sat on the dirt with my rifle on my lap. Curley waited on the other side of the barn behind a tall wagon. I sat, rubbing my sore legs, anxious and nervous for the sounds that would tell us that the catchers were coming. I had never been in a fight like the one I now faced. Doubts crept in and I worried about the outcome. Would I survive?

I shook the thoughts away and studied the repeating rifle, slowly working the action and imagining shooting and reloading by working the lever. I slid the spring forward and dropped the ejected shells back into the rifle one at a time, amazed at how simple it was. I looked toward the door to see the sun was gone and twilight lingered outside even as it grew steadily darker in the big barn.

My head jerked when I heard a man outside. He made no attempt to approach quietly, rather, he mumbled to himself and noisily threw the latch from the door and stepped inside. He stopped for only a second, but that second gave me a good opportunity to see that it was the man Curley had dropped to the dirt. He loosely carried a rifle in his right hand, but lowered it as he looked around and walked to the ladder leading to the loft where the prairie hay was stored. When he got there, I stepped out holding my rifle at my hip pointed at him. Oddly, he didn't look toward me, but turned his attention to the other side of the barn where a shot sounded. With incredible speed, he pointed the rifle and fired, then he turned to my standing place only fifteen feet away.

Of its own accord, my finger pulled the trigger and without conscious thought, I worked the lever and fired again. The man jerked twice and went to a knee. He looked at me with astonishment, then glanced to his unresponsive hands as if willing them to use the rifle and shoot.

Slowly, his arms lowered and the gun fell to the floor. He tried to speak but no sound came from his mouth, then, in unexpected slowness, he fell face first into the dirt. The dogs stood at the door, barking loudly, but they chose not to enter so I hurried to the man and bent to roll him over. His eyes stared lifelessly into the great beyond and I noticed with satisfaction, three bullet holes in his chest. I'd heard Curley's shot, but hadn't realized that his bullet, as well as both of mine, had found their mark. I picked up the man's rifle and backtracked to the stall in which I'd hid because the other slave catcher would certainly have heard the shots and come running.

Come running he did, but he was smart enough not to come barging through the door. Because the dogs occasionally looked over their shoulders in between their anxious barking, I suspected he was close.

"Kane? Kane, are you in there?"

Kane was inside, but he would never answer again. The dogs left the door and I could hear the man urgently try to shoo them away. It appeared his plan was to circle to the partially opened back door Curley and I had come through. As soundlessly as possible, I crept to that door and slipped through to crouch and hide behind a wide tree only five yards away.

I looked under a branch and saw only a part of his eyebrow as he cautiously peeked around the corner of the barn. When he didn't see anyone, he stepped boldly around, pointing his rifle toward the door I had only recently come through. My first thought was to step quickly around the tree with gun at the ready, but a sudden worry stopped me where I stood. I couldn't remember if I had chambered another bullet into my rifle after firing the second shot inside the barn. With a frown, I realized it would be suicide if I lurched from the tree only to pull the trigger on an already-fired bullet. I gritted my teeth. I could have chosen a less dangerous time to learn these lessons.

Leaning against the bark of the tree, I opened the lever as slowly as I could, but when the empty casing was thrown from the rifle, it made a clicking sound that seemed so loud it hurt my ears. I heard a sudden movement from the man so I rammed a new shell home and stepped in the open while bringing my gun to a shooting position.

His rifle was pointed to the other side of the tree. He had obviously expected me to come from there and his mistake saved my life, and cost him his. I quickly sent two marble-sized pieces of lead into his chest. As was the case with the first catcher, he jerked as each bullet hit him. He was able to get one shot off as he turned toward me, but the bullet harmlessly struck the big tree two feet from where I stood.

The man fell face down, hands outstretched on the ground. I breathed for a moment. It was the only thing I could do as I felt paralyzed. My muscles scarcely worked and I thought I would fall because of the most extreme weakness I'd ever felt. I thought perhaps I'd been hit, so in a hurried search, I ran my hand along my chest. I sighed in relief at finding no injury, but the exhaustion stayed with me. I swayed and felt like I'd pass out. Somehow I made my way to the side of the barn, leaning against it and sliding down to sit with splayed legs on the grass and weeds there. I had never killed a man, and although tremendously relieved that I had lived, the finality of the dead man before me crushed on my chest. I felt somehow.... tainted. My mind reasoned that I'd killed so as not to be killed, but the guilt hit me hard. For a full minute, I breathed and replayed the events of the last two minutes in my mind. With a jerk of my head, I remembered the shot Curley had fired. I looked up, fully expecting to see him standing over me, but I was alone.

I swallowed hard and jumped to my feet. "Curley?"

I rushed through the door and over to his hiding place. I couldn't see him in the encroaching darkness. I called again. "Curley?"

No sound. I ran from place to place, then stopped in dread when I saw his legs. I pushed into a narrow space where he'd fallen and knelt at his side to roll him from his stomach to his back. The hole in his broad chest and his blood-soaked shirt told me more than I wanted to know. I cradled his head in my arms and held it close to my chest. His eyes were closed and his expression, though I could take no solace, was peaceful.

"Oh, Curley."

Chapter 12

Full darkness enveloped the prairie before I was able to allow Curley's body to slide to the ground. He had been a good friend, my best friend, and now I was alone. I felt inadequate, but with all my soul, I vowed to continue our search and finish what we'd started. I wiped my eyes with the sleeve of my shirt, then stood and leaned on the wall in hopes that my aching knees would recover. At length, I gathered the rifle and made my way in the dark to the front door of the barn, then over to the slave catchers' cabin. There were things that needed done, and to do them, I needed a lantern.

The dogs, I suppose seeing me in charge and to my great relief, had stopped their barking and lay on the porch watching me. I let them be, hoping they would stay that way. I pushed the door open and stepped inside.

A small fire burned in a stove and tiny shafts of light escaped from the cast iron firebox. A lantern hung from a wire in the middle of the room. I reached and took it down, then with a match from a box on a shelf, I lit the lantern and held it high. I was immediately gratified when I saw the ring of keys on the scarred, wooden table, for that had been my objective. I took the keys in one hand and the lantern in the other and strode out the door and stood on the porch looking toward the road.

"Boy?" I held the lantern high in hopes he could see. "Boy, it's all over. There's nobody here to hurt you anymore."

There was no sound. I frowned until I realized that the youngster couldn't tell me from the slave catchers. I jogged down the lane to the buggy, but he was nowhere to be found. Smart boy. I called again then held the lantern to my face so he could see it was me.

"It's me, young'un. You can come out from your hiding."

I turned at a sudden movement in the trees at the side of the road. The light from the lantern reflected the whites of his eyes as he cautiously approached. I held the lantern high and motioned for him to get into the buggy. When he was seated, I climbed in and took the reins to start the horse along.

We stopped at the slave cabin, jumped to the ground and stepped to the door. I gave the lantern to the boy while I tried key after key on the padlock. Finally, the last key opened it and I was able to take it from the hasp and throw it into the darkness. I pushed the door open and leaned into the room to see four scared men huddled on the floor in one corner. The stench was overpowering and I quickly stepped back and put my hand over my face.

"Come on out of there."

One by one the men came away, heads down, heavy lines in their faces showing fear and resignation. I placed my hand on a shoulder and the man cringed in terror. I released my grip and stepped back.

"It's all right. Them slave catchers won't hurt you anymore." I held the ring of keys forward.

He studied the keys then looked at me, afraid to take

them in case it was a trick. I could understand his mistrust. Had I been in his place, I suspect I'd have felt the same. He licked his lips then turned to the boy who nodded in verification of what I'd said. A thin hand reached out and tentatively took the keys, but the man held them for a long time as if unsure of what to do.

I could see it was my presence that made him so nervous so I backed away while pointing to the remaining men. "Unlock everyone then come over to the other cabin and let's get you something to eat." I turned and strode to the cabin without a backwards glance.

The dogs relaxed on the porch, their rope-like tails thumping against the plank floor. They seemed unconcerned that their previous owners were no longer in charge and by all accounts now accepted me as their new master. I waited on the porch, talking calmly to them so when the men came they would allow them inside.

I heard talking and noticed the swinging lantern approaching. When the men stepped to the porch, the dogs growled but stopped at my reprimand. I motioned for everyone to enter and I followed to join the men standing around the rough-cut wooden table. I took the lantern from the boy and set it on a shelf attached to a post in the center of the room, then pointed left and right. "Y'all find something to eat, then we need to get ourselves back to Kansas."

It took a moment of indecision, but soon one man began pulling foodstuffs from a shelf at the side of the wood-burning stove and cutting strips of meat from a hanging side of venison against the back wall. The others stood and watched as the designated cook began frying the meat in a cast iron skillet.

I hadn't planned on staying long enough for a cooked meal because there was no telling how long before the businessman I'd left shackled at the road would be rescued.

But after seeing the gaunt and sunken faces of the men and boy, I decided the risk was worth it.

While the cook and the boy stayed busy at the stove, I grabbed another lantern and motioned for the rest of the men to follow me to the barn where I instructed two of them to hitch the mules to the wagon. The biggest man and I had the most unpleasant task. We lifted Curley and carried him to the wagon bed where we pushed him in. I wouldn't leave him in Missouri. He'd been a free man back home, and he deserved to be buried in the free soil of the Kansas prairie.

My plan was to get the former slaves safely across the line and far enough into Kansas so the catchers wouldn't be able to find them, then I'd take Curley back to Lawrence to be buried next to Mr. Grunwald. When that unpleasant business was taken care of, I would resume my expedition.

I took the rifles, one from the businessman and two that had until recently belonged to the slave catchers, and carried them to the buggy while the mule team and wagon, with Curley's and my horses tied to the back, were driven to the open space next to the cabin. By that time the cook and boy had a huge pan full of fried meat and onions ready for us to eat. We all stood around the table plucking the food from the pan with our hands and eating without restraint.

I ate several chunks but could see the men needed the meal much more than me. When finished, I licked the grease from my fingers then wiped my hands on my pants. I looked up to see the boy watching me intently. I cocked my head and shrugged. "What?"

His large eyes blinked hard, then he passed me a small jar. I took it and heard the unmistakable sound of coins rattling inside the glass. I lifted the top and peered inside to see several folded paper bills which I pulled out. I recognized a number of dollar bills like I'd seen the Grunwalds use at Mr. Smithson's store, but there were other bills also. I held one up to the lantern and read, CONFEDERATE STATES OF

AMERICA.

I frowned and threw them to the table, then swallowed when I saw at least ten golden eagles at the bottom of the dish. My first thought was that I couldn't take them because they didn't belong to me, but I quickly overcame that notion. The dead men at the barn certainly didn't need the money, and it had likely come from their chosen profession of slave catching. I glanced at the men still surrounding the table working diligently on the dwindling meat in the large bowl. If the money belonged to anyone, it should be them. I dumped the coins into my hand and shoved them and the bills deep into my pocket. Once in Kansas, I'd send them on their way with money for their future, knowing full well that no amount of money could make up for their past.

I looked up and realized the men had stepped back from the table and were looking at me. I shook the dark thoughts from my head and waved my hand around the cabin. "Take whatever you can use, clothes, hats, boots. Them catchers won't need them." I watched their faces and wondered if they'd understood. They seemed like little children, needing to be told what to do and when to do it. I motioned again. "Go ahead, but we need to hurry and get on the road."

They looked at one another, then with a nod from the cook, two left through the door while the others fanned out and looked through the cabin for anything of use. Within a couple of minutes, the men gathered their meager spoils and stepped to the porch. I followed and saw the two from outside, each with a pair of boots and a hat, obviously from the dead men. Without speaking, the cook nodded toward the wagon and each man climbed aboard.

I drove the buggy in the lead while the wagon followed behind in painstaking, mule-paced slowness. We turned west at the main road with hopes of reaching Spring Hill by morning. I realized we were in a precarious situation with slave catchers in front and behind, but if we could slip through in the night, perhaps we could find help in Kansas.

A bright, full moon rose to our rear and I cursed the bad luck. We had far to travel and I would have liked to have done so in darkness, but it was not to be. If we were found, the men now riding in the wagon would be robbed again of their chance for freedom, and I, who'd killed two men and stolen a buggy and wagon to help slaves escape, would like as not be hanged on the spot. I stood in the buggy and turned to look over the fringed top, dismayed at the almost daytime brightness that covered the road and landscape. I shook my head. All I could do was keep my eyes peeled, pay attention and hope for the best.

But after the day's events, keeping my eyes open proved difficult. I found my head bobbing in not-to-be-denied weariness. I jumped in fright when one of the men from the wagon jogged ahead and climbed into my buggy. He gently took the reins from my fingers and slapped them on the horse. It was only then that I realized we had stopped on the road. I nodded my appreciation, then let my chin rest on my chest.

Sometime in the night, I woke with a start, but relaxed when I recognized all was well. I was happy to see that Lady Luck rode with us. We saw nary another soul on the road. We crossed the border, then after a time turned north toward Spring Hill. As the first rays of the morning sun touched our right shoulders, I could see the tree tunnel that would take us past Jacob's place and into the town of Spring Hill.

I looked at the driver, noticing his eyes scarcely open. I reached for the reins and no sooner had them in my hand than he hung his head in sleep. I peered ahead, thinking. The horse and mules were undoubtedly wore out. We could stop in Spring Hill, but I questioned what I might expect when I rolled in with a wagon full of former slaves. I thought of our visit two days earlier. At that time, I had wondered if Spring

Hill was like Lawrence, openly against slavery, but even after our time there, I didn't know how they would react. I frowned as I contemplated the possibility of slave catchers in the town. It was, after all, very close to the Missouri line. The only other possibility was to find a way off the road and conceal ourselves in the woods. I pulled on the reins and stood in the buggy, leaning out under the top. There were many places to hide, but in hiding, we would be in danger of attack from any slave catchers who might stumble upon us. I looked toward the town, then back to the woods. Finally, I got down and walked to the wagon.

I pointed ahead. "We are coming to the town of Spring Hill. It's in Kansas so there are no slaves, but," I paused, "I've been told there are slave catchers about. We have two choices, either find a place to hide here in the woods or go into town and hope we can find some help." I knew that either possibility had risks, and I wanted the men with the most to lose to make the choice.

The cook rubbed his face with both hands, then glanced quickly at each of the others. No one spoke, but he looked at each before he reached a decision. He peered at me with a grim face. "Hide in the woods."

I had come to expect short answers. We'd spent our time together and I found them to be much like me, with little inclination to talk unless it was necessary. I nodded. "Very well."

We found what looked to be an old wagon trail leading from the road. It was overgrown, but no so thick as to prevent us from taking it deep into the tall trees. When we found a stopping place next to a small stream, we allowed the horses and mules to drink and graze, then left the boy with the animals while the rest of us went back to brush out the tracks and remove any sign as best we could.

Since I had been able to steal a few moments of sleep, I took the first watch while everyone else crawled under the wagon. I sat in the seat in the shade of a giant oak tree with my rifle across my knees and stared with heaviness at Curley's body, which lay in the wagon with a blanket from the catcher's cabin covering him. I thought of our time together, of his teaching and reassurance. In life, he'd never once asked anything of me, but in death I felt his encouragement for me to get the slaves to freedom. That was his way, to always be thinking about others. I took a deep breath and vowed to get the men farther north where they would be safe.

By midmorning, one rolled from under the wagon and climbed into the box to relieve me on watch. I wordlessly passed him one of the rifles, then skipped down to catch and saddle my horse. I wanted to go into Spring Hill to see what I could learn.

I slid one of the extra rifles into the scabbard and mounted, then with a wave at the sentry, turned and pushed through the brush. I stopped to look around as I got to the road, but saw no one. I rode through the tree tunnel and at my first sight of Spring Hill that morning, I knew it was an anti-slavery town just like Lawrence because, just like Lawrence, it had been burned and looted sometime since Curley and I had left only two days before.

I approached the outskirts and I saw Jacob's house under the big tree with the five-year-old standing on the walkway staring at me. The flowers had been trampled and the picket fence torn down and dragged away. Yet they were more fortunate than many because their house had not been burned. The green painted screen door opened quickly and Jacob's wife jerked her son inside and slammed the door. I shook my head as I leaned forward and kicked the horse along. He stepped lively and I trotted into town, swiveling my head back and forth to see the damage. The store had been burned as had the eatery across the street. Occasionally people peered at me from behind a post or from inside a partially burned building, but no one came out to greet me.

I saw the store owner who'd warned me about the slave catchers. For the thousandth time, I regretted my carelessness. He had warned me, but I hadn't taken his advice as seriously as I should have. I turned my horse to where he stood under the shade of an overhanging tree.

"Howdy."

He nodded but chose not to speak.

I waved my hand. "What happened here?"

"It was Quantrill and his gang of cutthroats. Came in at daybreak, shootin' up the town, lootin' what they could and burnin' the rest. The town's done for. Folks is already packin' up to leave for the north. It's too dangerous to stay around these parts."

I turned in the saddle to see the damage again, shaking my head at the senselessness of it all. When I turned back to the storekeep, he rubbed his chin.

"Where be your boy?"

It took me a moment to realize he was asking about Curley. I sighed, but it sounded more like a grunt. "Killed by some slave catchers across the line."

He grimaced. "Sorry to hear that. One of these days them slavers will get their comeuppance."

I nodded. "Those two already did." I let out a heavy breath. I was finished talking. There was nothing more to say and nothing more for me to see in Spring Hill. I turned my horse back toward the tree tunnel and the waiting men in the woods. We would hide for the rest of the day, then head for Lawrence after dark. If I could get the men there, I was sure the folks would help them along their way.

The afternoon slowly turned to evening. Slightly before dark we hitched the buggy and wagon, then tied the two horses to the back of the wagon. There was no way to skirt the settlement, so we made no effort to do so. Rather, we pushed through after darkness had closed in on the town. It seemed deserted with only a few lights shining from the farthest houses. We saw no one and hoped that no one saw us, and after five miles, we began to breathe easier.

Around midnight, the woods began to give way to the wide-open prairie, I pulled the buggy to a stop at the bottom of a depression. Curley had been dead since the previous evening and it had become apparent that getting him all the way to the Grunwald's farm was unrealistic. But at least I had gotten him to the prairie and hoped he would understand. We had no shovels but used sticks from a nearby skeleton of a tree to dig a shallow grave. We carefully placed his body, covered it with the blanket and mounded the dirt. Tears unashamedly came to my eyes when the men and boy gathered and sang a sad tune. I stood for a long time staring at the grave, missing him more than I ever dreamed possible. It was only when a lone wolf howled in the distance and the men acted nervous, that I wiped my eyes, replaced my hat and climbed into the buggy.

Before daylight, we stopped at a buffalo wallow with a small grove of trees and hid the wagon and buggy as best we could. We were only a few miles from Lawrence but I wasn't excited about the idea of parading the men through town in the light of day. I told the men to stay hidden if they could, then saddled my horse and trotted toward Lawrence. Having chosen not to hunt, I was tired and beyond hungry. I pulled to a stop in front of Mr. Smithson's store and stepped to the dirt. I looked up and down the street in awe at the work the townsfolk had done in putting things back together after the raid of only a week before. The awning posts, overhang and boardwalk had been replaced where needed, and the insides of the stores had been gutted and were in the rebuilding stage.

Mr. Smithson swept dust from his front door in the early morning light, but stopped and looked at me as I stood there. He smiled broadly when he recognized me, then stepped from the boardwalk and extended his hand. "Hello Branson."

I shook his hand heartily. "Mr. Smithson."

He stepped back to the shade of the boardwalk and leaned on his broom. I suppose he could tell from my expression that I wanted something. He tilted his head. "You look about done in. What can I do for you?"

I appreciated his perceptiveness. Of all the people in Lawrence, he was the only one I could think of who I was willing to tell about the runaways. I scraped the dirt with my boot, nervous about asking him for help. I glanced up. "You remember Curley? I introduced you last week before we left town."

His eyebrows pulled down in thought. "The black man?"

"Yes, him." I pointed over my shoulder. "We had a run-in with some slave catchers in Missouri. They—." My voice cracked as the emotion overtook me in a sudden, crushing weight.

He stepped from the boardwalk and put a hand under my arm and grasped firmly. "Come on inside and sit for a spell." He supported me as I stepped up, then guided me into the store and to a chair.

I hadn't planned on telling the whole story, but he listened intently. Before long the words spilled from me like water from a pump. When finished, I stared at the wood plank floor for a long time. I felt drained, like I had nothing left and couldn't go on.

Finally, I peered to Mr. Smithson. "I promised Curley I'd get the slaves away from Missouri and to safety in the north, but I've done about all I can do on my own. They are tired and hungry and need help. I didn't know where else to turn."

He stood and placed a hand on my shoulder. "You done good, Branson." He waved his hand toward the outside. "Some of us here in Lawrence have experience getting runaways to the north."

I jerked back in surprise. "Who?"

A mild shake of his head was my answer and I immediately regretted asking the question. "Sorry, that was out of line."

"No matter. The point is that we can do it, but I need you to stay with them a little longer." He motioned with his head for me to follow him to the back of the store where he had saved anything that hadn't been burned in the raid. He made a sack out of a square of cloth and placed crackers and apples inside before tying it with a string.

"Take these back to the men. It ain't much of a meal, but it's better than nothing." He scratched his jaw in thought. "At midnight I'll meet you at the Grunwald's. Nobody will be around and I'll take them from there." His eyes seemed to smolder like hot coals. "And Branson."

"Yes, sir."

"Never a word about any of this to anyone."

With a nod of agreement and thanks, I took an apple from the bin and walked out of the store to my horse.

Mr. Smithson held the bag until I mounted, then he passed it up. "You be careful."

"I will. Thanks. See you at midnight."

He leaned back and folded his ample arms and watched me turn and ride back the way I'd come.

The men set the bag on the wagon when I passed it down. With string untied, they slowly spread the cloth and looked at the contents. The cook, who had taken over as the leader of the group, passed crackers and apples to everyone, including me. We ate in knowing stillness, thankful for the meager meal.

At sundown, we hitched the animals and started the trip to the Grunwald's. No one spoke and the only sounds to be heard were the footfalls of the animals and the creaking of the wagon. The moon rose and bathed the prairie in silver light, but it was a light less frightening than the moonrise over Missouri.

The buggy horse and mules plodded along with heads down and swinging from side to side. I fought the urge to hurry them along. We were making good time and if all went well, I'd be headed back to Missouri by morning. The purpose for the trip remained the same, but my attitude had changed considerable. The past week had changed me. I was no longer the innocent boy I'd been. I had been shot at, returned fire and killed two men, and had lost my best friend in the process. I longed to be back in Missouri and I vowed to find and kill the men who had caused me so much grief. Slow and steady was a thing of the past for me. I would be careful, but when the time for action arrived, I'd be ready. The men I hunted didn't know me, yet, but they would soon enough.

When we approached the Grunwald's place, I pulled to a stop and motioned for the men to follow me into the fields. We picked ears of corn and ate until our bellies could hold no more. When we arrived at the burned house, I saw Mr. Smithson waiting. He stood alone and I couldn't see a horse or buggy.

"Whoa." I jumped down and shook his hand, then stepped to the side of the wagon. I looked at the men while motioning to the store keep. "This here is Mr. Smithson. He's going to get you to the north." I reached into my pocket and pulled out the bills and double eagles, then reached over the side and let everything slip from my hand. The heavy coins thudded as they hit the boards. I made sure Mr. Smithson leaned over to see.

"This is money the slave catchers got from selling slaves." I motioned toward the men. "It belongs to them. Will you please make sure they get it when they reach the north?"

He nodded. "Mighty generous of you."

I shrugged. "Weren't my money to begin with. They'll need something to get a start."

Smithson leaned again to look at the coins, then reached inside to grasp one before turning to me. "What about you?"

I made a face. "What about me?"

He rubbed the stubble on his chin, then held the heavy coin and studied it in the moonlight. Finally, he looked up. "Don't you think you'll need something to get a start?" He held his hand out, palm up with the double eagle clearly visible.

The dull, reflected light held my attention. It wasn't my money and I'd never had any intention of keeping any of it. From my perspective, it was dirty money made from the suffering of others. I gazed into Smithson's face. "I'll make do."

He shook his head and placed a beefy hand on my shoulder. "We'll make sure these men get to the north and this money will be given to them when they get there, but... ."

"But what?"

"But... ," He paused again and looked to each of the men in the wagon before turning to me. "But I can see from your eyes that you are heading out. I don't know where or why, but I'll not send you away with empty pockets. It's a mighty cruel world out there and I insist that you take this twenty-dollar gold piece to get you started to wherever you are going. I've watched you Branson. You've had your share of troubles, but you are a young man who will make his mark on this land." He waved toward the men and boy. "You've made a difference in the lives of these men and I'm sure they won't begrudge you one double eagle in repayment." He leaned forward and dropped the coin into my shirt pocket, then patted my chest.

I pursed my lips. I'll admit that I had been concerned about my penniless trip back to Kansas. I couldn't reasonably expect help along the way, and realized that at some point I'd need money to buy food or supplies. Green field corn might keep me from starving, but it wouldn't provide the strength I was sure I'd need to track down the murderers. I looked at the men, their dark faces barely visible as a cloud obscured the moon. I turned to the cook, who seemed to be the man the others looked to when a decision was to be made.

The moonlight reflected on his teeth as he smiled. "That be right, sir. You done us right. It only be fittin' we do you the same."

I took a deep breath, unsuccessfully trying to drive out the pain in my chest for what they'd gone through, as well as for me at Curley's loss. He was no longer around to guide me, which meant I'd have to make it on my own. I was young, too young, but I'd seen and done things that had aged me considerable. Still, I was afraid of failure. I knew what I wanted to accomplish, but deep down, my doubts were ever-present. Who was I but a dumb kid with no family, no experience and only a small chance of surviving the coming ordeal? I reached for a parting shake.

The cook tentatively took my hand in both of his and squeezed. I knew he was on his way to freedom, to a new life. I was happy I'd been able to help.

He squeezed one last time. "Thank you, sir, for all you done."

I hurried to the back of the wagon and untied my horse because I didn't want Mr. Smithson to see the glistening in my eyes. I slipped the rifle into the scabbard and mounted, then turned with a wave of goodbye and loped toward Missouri.

Randall Dale

Chapter 13

By noon I reached the depression where we'd buried Curly. I unsaddled to let the horse roll, then I hobbled him for a chance to graze. I stood at the grave with my hat in my hand. I wanted to tell Curley about getting the slaves to Mr. Smithson, but I guessed he already knew. I wondered again how Curley had been able to get to the Grunwald's as a runaway slave all those years earlier, especially after hearing the comment from Mr. Smithson about how folks around Lawrence knew something about getting slaves to the north. I decided that when my quest was complete, I'd go back and ask the questions I'd always wished Curley would have answered.

The shade of a wild walnut tree next to the small stream gave me a chance to rest. I lay on my back with my hat over my eyes, expecting to sleep only a few minutes, but when I awoke, the sun touched the horizon. I rolled up with a start, embarrassed that I'd allowed myself such indulgence. I relaxed when I saw the horse grazing where I'd left him and decided that the sleep for me and the rest and grazing for him had been exactly what we'd needed.

With the slowness of a man near starvation, I removed the hobbles and re-saddled for our southward journey. I rode into the night, toward the town of Spring Hill, all the while thinking about the delicious meal Curley and I had eaten there only a few short days earlier. There would be no meal there for me on this trip even though I had money in my pocket because Spring Hill, like Lawrence, was in ruins.

Judging from the moon, I guessed it was around midnight when I rode through. As before, the town was dark with no one about. That suited me fine because there was no one there I wanted to see, but I did take a longing look at the shell of the eatery before kicking into a trot past Jacob's house and into the tree tunnel beyond. I rode for another hour, and in crossing a stream, allowed the horse to drink while I knelt, dipping my hand into water and bringing it to my mouth because that's what Curley had taught me to do when times called for care. In the moonlight I saw an overgrown path through the trees. I followed it to a small meadow where I unsaddled and hobbled the horse, keeping him close to warn me if anyone happened to find my camp. I fell asleep the minute my head rested against the smooth seat of the saddle.

The early morning sounds of the woods coming alive woke me from a deep sleep. My head hurt and I barely had the strength to roll to my knees and stand. If I didn't get something to eat soon, I would never make it to Harrisonville.

In only a few minutes, I made it to the junction where I took the east road toward Missouri. In another hour, I pulled the horse to a stop at the sign indicating the state line. I gazed ahead, into the state where destiny awaited. I swallowed hard, and realizing what lay ahead, I allowed myself a moment of self-doubt.

I shook my head in aggravation and kicked forward,

riding numbly ahead, past the place where the slave catcher had taken my boots, and along the dusty road toward the cabins and barn where I'd killed the men.

The clearing appeared much sooner than I'd expected. When walking with no boots, it had seemed longer than ten miles, but the trip on horseback had been fast and easy. I pulled to a stop, The tall corn waved in the afternoon breeze and as before, I noticed with surprise that no one seemed to be working the crop.

My hand involuntarily turned the horse into the lane, the thought of the fried venison strips we'd eaten drawing me in as though I had no will to resist. The dogs barked as I approached, but the door to the main cabin remained closed and I could see no movement inside.

"Hello the house."

No answer. Though my first inclination was to rush in and see what there might be to eat, I kicked the horse to the back of the barn to see if anyone had come to take care of the men. What I saw ruined my appetite. The dogs, with no one to feed them, had eaten the face and into the chest of the dead man under the tree. The sight, combined with the smell, made me gag. I put my hand to my mouth to stifle a heave and quickly turned away, coughing and shaking my head as I rode back to the cabin.

I sat in front for a time, watching the dogs lounging on the front porch while I tried to drive the disturbing image from my mind. Finally, I stepped down and into the cabin, walking directly to the hanging quarter of venison, for I needed meat. I pulled my knife and cut away the dried, crusted outer bark, then cut cubes of meat and shoved them into my mouth one at a time, chewing slowly, savoring the gamy taste.

I pulled a chair and sat next to the table, breathing deep in resting exhaustion. It took a full thirty minutes before I felt I had the strength to stand and look through the shelves next to the wood-burning stove. There was coffee, flour, sugar and a tin of molasses. I looked around the cabin and decided to stay the night. After all, it didn't look like anyone else was planning on staying, so I put my horse in the barn and fed him good with prairie hay from the loft, then returned to the cabin with an armload of wood from the lean-to.

The small fire in the stove quickly warmed the coffee and I poured the hot liquid into a tin cup along with enough sugar to make it sweet. I cooked and ate more meat and washed it down with the coffee until I had to unbutton my pants because of my extending belly.

Two beds occupied the east side of the cabin so I kicked off my boots and lay on one with my hands behind my head. Then, at a sudden thought, got up and cut more meat and threw it out to the dogs for their supper.

I was up before dawn, and after another meal of fried meat and sweetened coffee, I saddled and rode toward Harrisonville. As I got closer, I noticed the farms grew more numerous and I occasionally saw people on the road. Because of my previous experience with Missourians, I was surprised at their cheery expressions and pleasant greetings. I occasionally saw slaves working in the fields and it seemed so contradictory to me that the white folks were so happy, when their property, the slaves, were far from it.

As I rode into town two hours before sundown, the sheer number of people and the size of the town amazed me. I had thought Lawrence was a big town, but Harrisonville made it look like a village. Houses were scattered around the outskirts of town, and tall, false-fronted business buildings lined both sides of the long main street as well as other streets to the left and right. I saw dry goods stores, banks, more saloons than I could count, lawyer's offices, a doctor's office, a blacksmith shop along with countless other smaller stores. People bustled about the town, women in and out of shops and men in and out of saloons.

I realized with a frown that I hadn't thought out exactly how I'd find the murderers. I suppose in my mind I had expected to ride up to them and start shooting. In instant dejection, I worried that I'd be able to find them at all. I could hardly go to the sheriff and ask about them. Curley had made that plain after I'd gone to Jacob's wife and couldn't understand why she didn't tell me everything I wanted to know. No, I'd need to find out about them without anyone suspecting I was looking, but I didn't know exactly the best way to do that.

I rode to a wood-sided water trough in front of a dry goods store and stepped down to allow my horse to drink while, with long, even strokes, I worked the hand pump to keep the trough full. A couple of horses were tied to the hitching rail in front of the store, but at least twenty horses stood in three-legged relaxation in front of the neighboring saloon.

A quick glance at the swinging doors showed a steady flow of traffic in and out of the place and I suddenly became aware of the raucous noise escaping into the street. I thought perhaps I could go in and listen for anyone to mention the names of those for which I searched, and hope to hear anything that might be valuable.

I'd no more than tied my horse to the rail when a man came hurtling out of the saloon, almost tearing the swinging doors from their hinges. He landed in a heap on the boardwalk, then rolled off and under the feet of the suddenly nervous horses. They set back and put a strain on the deep-set hitching rail. It held, but several of the reins broke and the horses shied back and into the street.

The man, short and squat with longish black hair plastered against his hatless head and several day's growth of a thick, black beard, rolled to his knees and stood, swaying slightly in inebriated unsteadiness. He looked toward the saloon doors and it was only then that I noticed another man walking onto the boardwalk from inside. The new man stood tall in a fringed, buckskin shirt and low crowned, black hat. He looked neither left or right, but concentrated on the man in the street with the most intense eyes I've ever seen. Seeing those eyes brought a shiver to my back, and he wasn't even looking at me.

They stared at each other for only a moment, then the street man reached for a pistol inside a covered holster. The man under the shade waited as his opponent fumbled his attempt to draw his weapon, then with a taunting smile, he calmly pulled a pistol from the front of his pants, pointed it and fired one fatal round.

The black-headed man jerked as a sudden, tiny hole appeared in the center of his chest. He blinked heavily, right hand still trying unsuccessfully to remove his pistol, then with no attempt to protect himself from the fall, he fell face down into the dust.

Men from the saloon cheered the action and slapped the victor on his back with comments showing their approval. Then all marched back into the saloon to continue their afternoon imbibing.

Most of the townsfolk barely glanced at the dead man in the street, rather, they went about their business as though killings in front of the saloon were common. The only quarter they gave was to walk wide around the sprawled figure.

"Who was it?"

I hadn't seen the young man stroll to my side and I jumped at the sudden question. I turned to him and saw a grimace of disgust under his trimmed moustache. His hair, blond, and parted in the middle, was also carefully combed with not so much as one lock out of place, and his round spectacles reflected the sunlight as he looked into the street.

I slipped my thumbs into my pockets and cocked my

head. "Don't know. I'm new in town. Got here just in time to see the shooting."

At the answer, he nodded, then, holding a small notebook in one hand, he licked the tip of the pencil in the other. "What's your name?"

"Branson Hawk."

I frowned as he wrote in the book. I didn't know who he was or why he would want to write my name. I took a step back. "What are you doing?"

"Interviewing you." He pointed down the street. "I'm Silas Solomon. I own the Harrisonville Journal." He cocked his head and his frown deepened. "When I heard the shot, I came to get the story." He turned to see the dead man while angrily pointing a long, slender finger. "This senseless killing has got to stop. This is the third one this week."

He took a deep breath and turned to me while still pointing his finger. I was sure a lecture was on its way, but when a man with a star pinned to his chest approached the body from the other side of the street, the newspaperman rushed out to learn the details of the killing.

I stood in the shade and watched for a moment, then blinked in concern when the Journal man pointed at me with his pencil. Both men immediately marched to where I stood.

The pencil waved again in my direction. "He said he saw the whole thing." He then licked the pencil tip again and poised to write.

The deputy studied me for a moment, then frowned and pointed over his shoulder with his thumb. "Well?"

"Well what?"

His exasperation came through in his voice. "Silas, here, says you saw the whole thing. Is that right?"

I looked to the dead man before glancing back to Silas and the deputy. "I suppose so."

The deputy tapped his foot in growing impatience. "And...?"

I shrugged. "The man got hisself shot and killed."

He puffed his chest, pulled his pants to his hips and stared at me with squinted, angry eyes. "I can see that. Are you going to tell me what happened or do I need to lock you up until your memory improves?"

I didn't know much about the law, but I was mostly certain he couldn't throw me into jail for minding my own business. But the threat hung in the air like a bad smell and I had no reason to make the deputy mad. I raised my hands, palms up. What would it matter if I told what I'd seen? I told the story from the first to the last. He seemed impressed that I could describe the killer in detail, from the top of his hat to the heels of his boots. I smiled inwardly. Observation had become second nature.

The deputy nodded. "I'm guessing the killer jumped on his horse and headed out?"

I shook my head. "Nope, turned around and went back in the saloon."

The deputy angrily jutted his chin toward me. "Why didn't you tell me that in the first place?" Without waiting for an answer he marched into the saloon with the newspaperman close behind.

The killing had nothing to do with me so I watched them go, but my boyish curiosity got the better of me and I strolled to the batwing doors and leaned to see inside. The deputy sat in a chair with Silas standing at his shoulder. Across from them, the killer slouched in the chair, long legs sprawled under the table and one arm over the chair back. He smiled in relaxed friendliness.

He and the deputy talked, then the lawman turned to other men standing close. They readily nodded their heads in affirmation to whatever the killer had told the deputy, then the tall man in the buckskin jacket looked again to the deputy with an expression of unworried satisfaction. The men had obviously agreed that he'd shot in self-defense and he now had nothing to fear from the law. Silas shook his head as he furiously scribbled on his pad, then he stopped when the deputy stood and pointed to the door.

Even in the street I could feel the hush of the crowd. The killer had obviously been ordered out of the saloon, and possibly from the town. His eyes turned cold as he squinted, but as fast as that expression had come, it was replaced with an easy smile and he shrugged. He pushed up from the chair and waved cheerily to the men, then strolled in exaggerated calmness to where I stood.

Our eyes met as I backed away from the doors and he pushed through. He was a big man, with broad shoulders and taller than me by three or four inches. His forced smile was gone and his pockmarked face burned red in fury. I knew then that his calmness had been an act. I felt cold all over as he paused to study me. His eyes narrowed and I felt fear. If I hadn't been leaning against the building, I would have taken another step back just to be farther away.

His scrutiny of me passed as quickly as it had come. He turned away, ignoring me as one might a snake after realizing it was not a cottonmouth and therefore not dangerous. He stepped around the hitching rail and jerked a slipknot of not one, but two horses. He mounted and turned the horses to the street before glancing past me to the saloon doors and nodding. I turned to look, expecting to see the deputy, but it was someone else. The new man nodded, then turned back into the saloon.

The gunshot was as loud as it was unexpected. I jerked in surprise, then watched as the new man bolted out the door and vaulted into the saddle. With a shout, both men spurred their horses into a dead run out of town.

Additional shouts came from the saloon so I stepped to peer over the doors. I saw Silas, his face ashen, his mouth agape. I followed his gaze to see the deputy on the floor, blood soaking his shirt and running in a small rivulet along the wood slats. I stared in astonishment.

Men rushed to the deputy, forcefully pushing Silas away. He dropped his notepad and pencil and sank into a chair in shock. To this day I don't know why I did it, but he looked so frail in his frilly white shirt and string tie. I pushed through the doors, then stooped to pick up his pad and pencil. He watched with complete detachment as I took his arm and helped him to stand. I guided him through the doors and turned right when I recalled his pointing to his newspaper shop. I held his arm as we walked along the boardwalk, then as we reached a hand-painted sign announcing THE HARRISONVILLE JOURNAL, I opened the door, gently pushed him through and into a chair behind a desk while I sat in one on the other side.

He breathed deeply for a full minute until the shock began to wear off. He looked at me and licked his lips. "Thank you."

I shrugged. What could I say?

He reached for his notepad which I'd placed on the desk. Flipping through the pages, he stopped, read for a short moment and looked to me. "The dead man's name was Wilbur Cowan."

I jolted up. It was a name I'd had on the tip of my tongue since learning it from Jacob. I let the revelation sink in and mentally crossed that name off the list, glad that I'd been there to see it and know of a certain that he'd been sent to the devil, for that was surely where he belonged. My list now held only two names.

Silas seemed to have come to himself. He looked at me, obviously curious about my reaction to the name.

I rubbed my palms together and looked at the floor for a moment. The less anyone knew about my search, the better. I glanced up. "Never seen the man."

Whether he believed me or not, I couldn't tell. I could see he wanted to question more and I suppose that was the newspaperman coming out in him. As for me, I'd come to do a job and now I searched for two instead of three.

He flipped a page in the book. "And the odd thing was that they were friends. He and the killer, I mean. They returned from Kansas only two days ago. A man in the saloon said they'd ridden together as part of Quantrill's militia. According to the men there, it was a petty argument, one of no consequence until Cowan pushed too far."

I sat up, interested in the rest of the story. "And the killer's name?"

He looked at his book again. "Cleatus Frye."

I coughed in a feeling of sudden inadequacy. I had dreamt of facing the man, of pointing my rifle and pulling the trigger as he watched me with full understanding of my reason. But the dreams of a boy do not stand up to the realities of facing a murderer. I stood from the chair, turned and walked to the window, staring out with swirling remembrances of my family and the Grunwalds who'd been killed by him. I suppose my resolve should have built, and in my anger, I should have ran to my horse and chased after them, but all I could do was remember the chill in my chest when he turned to me outside the saloon.

I swallowed hard in instant dejection. Who was I trying to fool? How could I, a lone plowboy from Kansas, hope to track down and face such ruthless killers? I knew without doubt that they would put me in the ground without so much as a second thought.

From somewhere inside me the shame for my fear welled up and tried to whip my courage from its hiding place. I thought of the slave catchers I'd bested and for a moment, daydreamt of making Cleatus Frye pay for his crimes, but any bravery I felt dwindled at the realization that the slave catchers were tenderfeet compared to the man in the buckskin shirt. I sighed and cursed my cowardice, but no amount of silent screaming at myself could make my feet move to the door.

I hung my head in shame. I had promised myself that I would avenge the deaths of those I loved, but I shrank from the task, and with resignation, realized that I was no match for the Frye brothers and they would go unpunished. I took a deep breath, accepting the fear, taking it in until it uncomfortably filled every space in my body, and with that fear, came to terms with myself that one of the outlaws was dead and perhaps that hoping for more was a dream I could no longer keep alive. What was done was done, and there was nothing more I could do.

I turned to the newspaperman. "I've got to go." Without another word, I opened the door and shuffled to my horse, mounted and turned west. Perhaps I could go back to Lawrence. I could get a job and be all right.

I turned and looked back over my shoulders to where the Frye brothers had run. I shook my head in self-disgust, then kicked the horse into a steady trot toward home.

Chapter 14

The rider came racing through the town of Lawrence at breakneck speed, screeching at the top of his lungs. "The war is over. The war is over."

I leaned on the broom on the boardwalk in front of Mr. Smithson's store and peered out as the dust from the racing horse swirled through the town. Townsfolk came boiling out of the shops and stores in excited exhilaration. We'd heard rumors that the end of the long, bloody conflict was near, and nobody wanted the end more than those of us who'd lived through the constant threat to Eastern Kansas of more killing and looting from the marauders claiming to be Confederate soldiers. The raids had diminished since the Union army had pushed the rebels back to the south, but those of us from Lawrence who'd lived through the early raids knew that the mob could be into town, burn and loot, then be away before anyone could hardly fire a shot.

I rushed into the store. "Mr. Smithson, the war is over!" I leaned the broom to the counter and pulled the string at the back to untie my apron, then ran to the street to join the spur-of-the-moment celebration. Men clapped each other on their backs while women smiled in unrestrained exuberance.

I stayed in the street in the midst of the celebration for only a while and the joy at the news slowly dissipated because my thoughts turned to how much the war had cost me. I'd lost a Ma, a Pa, brothers and sister, and a best friend, although Curley's death wasn't a direct result of the war. But not a day went by that I didn't think of him. He'd tried to teach me, to get me ready to hunt the marauders, but when my chance came, I'd been too afraid to keep my promise. In my shame I never told anyone, not even Mr. Smithson, who had cared for me that year and a half, let me work in his store, fed me at his table and allowed me to live in a little lean-to attached to the side of the building. I kept to myself and lived daily with the knowledge and disgrace of my cowardice.

In the weeks that followed the announcement of the war's end, returning soldiers drifted into town, some to jubilant celebrations that they'd made it home safely to their families, others to burned out homesteads and cold headstones of loved family members. In my mind, the tiniest ember of hope remained in me that my Pa might come shuffling into town. I worked in the store and watched the street at every opportunity in case he happened by, but as the weeks turned to months, the little ember slowly faded to nothingness. I was alone, afraid and ashamed.

The months turned into a year and I said hello and goodbye to my seventeenth birthday. Although I'd reached my full height and the muscles in my arms grew to rival Curley's, I lived in daily realization that I was a coward. I kept to myself, a loner in every sense of the word, only interacting with others when forced to do so when Mr. Smithson was away from the store.

Then, as the oppressive heat of late summer came with a vengeance to eastern Kansas, something happened that I couldn't explain. I'd been straightening canned goods on the shelves when my attention was drawn to a stranger wearing a tattered Union uniform. The sight was not altogether uncommon, for many of the veterans who'd returned, especially those who's homesteads had been burned in the looting, had nothing more to wear. The man rode a flop-eared mule to the front of the store and slid off, straightened to his full height and looked up and down the street. He took a deep breath and wearily climbed the steps to the boardwalk, then with a sigh, strolled into the store. Mr. Smithson glanced up to see him enter. He hurried from the counter and pushed a stool to the man.

"Howdy, sir."

The old soldier nodded in greeting. "Afternoon."

He stood at his full height, which was considerable. He was thin with a huge Adam's apple that bobbed as he talked. Deep lines etched his face and his old, gray beard was ragged, but his eyes were bright and he smiled as Mr. Smithson grasped his bony knuckles. In slow movement, he folded himself onto the stool, pulling his long legs to rest on the wooden railing underneath.

He placed his wide hands on his thighs. "Obliged." He then glanced at me, no, stared at me, studying me with deep, penetrating eyes.

I placed the feather duster on the counter and felt embarrassed at his scrutiny, but his expression lightened and his eyes danced under brushy eyebrows. A small smile came to his lips and he acknowledged me with a small wave of his hand. "Son."

"Sir."

He smiled more broadly and pointed west. "I'm heading toward Topeka."

Mr. Smithson pulled another stool from behind the counter and sat heavily facing the man. "You look like you're plumb tuckered out. If you've a mind, you are welcome to rest here for as long as you like."

The soldier rubbed the sides of his face and he blinked so slowly that when his eyes closed I thought he'd gone to sleep, but when he opened them, he gazed directly at me.

"How old you be, son?"

"Seventeen, sir."

He took a deep breath and let it out slowly while tilting his head, first to one side, then the other, all the while looking at me. "Seventeen-years-old. A good age." He glanced at Mr. Smithson, then leaned forward and returned his attention to me. "I saw many a young soldier your age in the war. So many of them showed up hankering for a fight, thinking themselves anxious for action and chomping at the bit to charge ahead. It only taken one volley from them reb guns to change their minds mighty fast. Some o' them young'uns what was acting the bravest were the first ones to turn tail and run for cover.

"Others come in admittin' they was scared. Them was the smart ones. The good Lord put it in every brave man to start out bein' scared. Gives a feller a chance to think about things, to plan and learn and grow and be ready for whatever fight comes his way."

I swallowed hard as his eyes bored into me. I didn't know why he stared at me and talked about fear. It was as if he'd known my confidence had been shattered and that I'd branded myself a coward. My mind raced and I blurted the question without thinking. "Were you ever afraid?"

His expression was serious, but he wasn't offended. Rather, he looked me straight in the eye. "I was scared every day. There ain't no shame in it. Fact is, being scared saved my life more than once because it made me cautious and aware." He paused for a moment and rubbed his palms on his pants. Finally, he looked at me again. "There be only one kind of fear, but there be two ways to deal with it. A man can run and never look back, or he can hold that fear until the time is right to move forward. A brave man is only a scared man who moves ahead with his plan."

My breath caught in my throat. In front of me sat the soldier, gray-haired, blue-eyed, tall and thin, but I swear I saw Curley, broad and thick with dark eyes staring at me. I heard his voice as though he was there at that moment teaching me.

I shook my head. No, it wasn't Curley, only an old soldier with nowhere to go and nothing to do. He couldn't know of my fear and even if he did, it was different. Cleatus Frye was a killer, plain and simple. I'd watched him gun a man down without any pretense of remorse and knew deep down that if I faced him he would do the same to me. I looked down and away, unable to bear the old man's inspection. He somehow had seen through me and knew my deepest secret, and I was ashamed.

A half-minute went by as I relived my fear. I wondered why the man had come and why he'd said what he did. It was a mystery to me, and the heavy weight that had pressed on me since my return to Lawrence pushed more firmly on my chest. All was quiet in the store except for the ticking of the old clock on the wall until the old man took a deep, raspy breath. Embarrassed that I'd allowed my thoughts to wander, I glanced up and looked from one man to the other. I nodded, then in shame, I stood and walked through the back of the store to my lean-to.

A day passed with the old man's words ringing in my ears. Those soldier boys had been afraid, I knew that, but they had others around them. I was all alone. I had every right to be afraid. Who could expect me not to be?

I sat on my bed in the light of the coal oil lamp. Everywhere I looked, all I could see was Curley's face staring at me repeating the same words the old soldier had spoken. Sweat beaded on my lip and I looked up and blinked at a sudden realization. It had been there all along but in my self-pity, I hadn't recognized it. My fear had possibly saved my life. If not for those feelings at that time, I might have chased after the killers and met the same fate as the man in the street.

The room seemed to brighten as I recalled what the old solder said about fear making a man cautious so he could grow and plan. It began to make sense.

For the first time since my return, I thought about my fear in a different way. Might the old soldier have been right? Could it be that mine was a healthy fear, a protective fear, one to be used for good and not one to cause inaction? I chewed my lip at another thought. He'd said fear held no shame. Could that be true? Had my fear allowed me to grow and mature so I'd be ready to face my future?

Slowly, the burden of my fright lifted as I realized that in Harrisonville, it had been a natural reaction of a mere boy. I was now seventeen and unexpectedly, the vision of the murderer did not cause me to shrink away.

I thought of the promise I'd made to Curley to make the outlaws pay for what they'd done to both our families. My breast swelled with instant warmth. I could see it so plainly, I'd been too young to challenge killers as ruthless as the Frye brothers. I swallowed. I was older, bigger and stronger, and, possibly even wiser. Might it be possible that I had matured enough to face my fear? I looked at the floor in thought and decided the answer was yes. With determination borne from the wise soldier's words, I, then and there, decided to keep that promise no matter what, and I would use my fear as an ally rather than as the demon in my chest that had caused me shame.

I stooped to reach under the bed where my fingers found the Henry repeating rifle that I'd placed out of sight after returning to Lawrence. I sat and held the rifle on my lap, brushing the long-accumulated dust from its face. The time had come for me to use the rifle, and use it, I would.

I pulled two quarters from a jar above the bed, clinking them together, flipping one over the other with my fingers. Starting tomorrow, I thought, I'd start preparations for the day I would meet Cleatus and Rastus Frye.

The next morning I took the coins and pushed them across the counter to Mr. Smithson. He took them from the wood and studied them for a few seconds.

"What are these for?"

"A box of shells." It was to be the first of many boxes, and every day over the next month, I took the rifle to the prairie to practice and plan.

The date I'd chosen finally arrived. I pulled my hat low and slipped the rifle into the scabbard and two boxes of shells into the saddlebag. Mr. Smithson reached over the horse to shake my hand. I grasped it and gave it a heartfelt squeeze.

"Thanks you for all you done."

He shook his head. "My pleasure."

I hadn't told him of my plans or the reason I was leaving. The last thing I needed was someone trying to talk me out of starting my search. All he knew was that since the visit of the old soldier, I had changed.

I mounted and looked down at him. His eyes rested on me for a moment, then he slapped my thigh.

"Good luck, Branson."

"Thank you." I gave the horse his head and rode down the street and into the prairie beyond. The horse, the same one that had carried me to Missouri a lifetime ago, tugged at the bit, anxious to go, so I allowed a smooth, half-trot that would eat the miles but not make him too tired.

By nightfall I reached Spring Hill, happy to see most of the buildings rebuilt and the little town thriving. I stopped and ate a filling meal at the eatery, sitting by myself while listening to any conversation for hints of the whereabouts of the brothers Frye. Hearing none, I paid for the meal and rode south until I could find a place to leave the road and sleep for the night.

My destination was Harrisonville in hopes that someone there would know the whereabouts of the men I sought. I jogged into the city during an afternoon downpour. Water ran from the roofs to the street, causing a small river to flow through the town. I rode directly to the storefront with HARRISONVILLE JOURNAL painted in gold letters on the window. It was admittedly a long shot, but the owner, if he was still around, had shared information with me previously, perhaps he might again.

I stepped onto the dryness of the boardwalk, slapping my hat against my pants to knock some of the water away from both. The rain pounded on the roof as I looked through the glass to see the owner sitting at the same desk where I'd left him those many months earlier. I shook myself in an effort to shed the rainwater, then opened the door and strolled through with my hat in my hand.

He glanced up from his reading and cocked his head as he gazed at me. I suspected he recognized my face and searched his memory for my name. I was at the same disadvantage, for I knew he was the owner of the paper, but I couldn't remember his name either.

I hurried to the desk and reached across. "Branson Hawk."

He looked down as the drops from my sleeve splatted to the desk, but he smiled. "Silas Solomon." His eyes opened wide. "I remember now. You were here the day the deputy was killed in the saloon."

 "Yes, sir. I was hoping you'd remember me."

He chuckled. "As I recall, I was a bit shaken up that day. I stood next to the deputy when Rastus Frye gunned him down in cold blood. I thought he was fixing to shoot me too, that's what had me discombobulated." He stepped around the desk and offered to take my coat. I passed it to him so he could hang it on a coatrack by the front door where the drops could collect over some old newsprint placed there. He wiped the moisture from his hands on his pants while walking to a counter with wide drawers underneath. He pulled one, then started turning newsprint pages. After a time, he pulled one from the stack and brought it to the desk. "I remember his name because of the story I wrote." He tapped the paper. "Here it is."

I leaned and quickly read, careful not to let any water from my hair drip to the paper. I was impressed with the reporting. From my recollection, he told the story accurately. I nodded. "Yep, that's how I remember it."

He smiled and sat in the chair behind the desk, absently taking his spectacles and rubbing them vigorously with a cloth. He motioned to an empty chair. I sat, crossed my legs and placed my still-dripping hat on one knee. So far, he seemed anxious to talk about the events of that day. That had been my hope, for I determined that if anyone might know, or could find out where the brothers were, it would be the newspaperman.

He leaned forward to study me. "You were a might younger then."

"I was for a fact."

"So, what can I help you with today?"

I motioned toward the paper. "I'm only wondering where those Frye fellers are now?"

He leaned back in his chair and replaced his spectacles by pulling the curved springs behind his ears. "Last I heard they were running from the law down south somewhere." He frowned. "Why do you want to know?"

I hesitated. It was nobody's business but mine why I wanted to know their location, but I also knew that unless I had some kind of answer, Silas would have no reason to help me. "A little unfinished business."

He leaned forward. "My reporter ears are hearing a story

in this. Tell me more."

I twirled my hat in my hands while trying to decide what I should and shouldn't tell. Of a certain, I didn't want him writing about my search, but I knew I needed help in locating the men, so I made the decision. "I'll tell you, but this is personal with me and you have to promise it won't ever come out in a story."

He looked disappointed. "Very well, but I'm interested all the same."

So I briefly told of the men raiding into Kansas and killing my family and how they'd also killed the Grunwalds. Although I could tell he wanted to hear more of the details, he'd heard all I was willing to tell. I sat on the edge of the chair. "I promised myself I'd make them pay, but I need to know where to find them. That's why I need your help."

He leaned with elbows on the desk, his fingers making a tent under his chin. I couldn't see his eyes because of the glare on his glasses, but he seemed to be thinking. I sat quietly, giving him time. At length, he leaned back and folded his arms. "You'll get yourself killed."

My lips pressed together. I had come to that same conclusion, accepted it, then dismissed it. Come what may, I was determined to press forward. "Possibly, but it's something I've got to do, and I'll do it with or without your help."

He raised his hands, palms out. "Hold on. I didn't say I wouldn't help. I only wanted to know if you've thought of the possibilities."

"I have and my mind is made up."

"I see." He looked to a grandfather clock against the side wall. "Are you ready for a visit to the saloon?" He stood and pulled a derby hat from a rack at the side of his desk, then strode out the door with me following behind wondering how the saloon might help me find the raiders. We walked under the protection of the overhang all the way to the same saloon where I'd stood when the deputy had been killed.

Silas strode directly to the batwing doors, paused only long enough to smile at me, then he walked directly to the end of the bar far away from anyone else in the saloon. I took the space next to him, leaning on the bar while placing one foot on the brass rail underneath. The bartender strolled our direction while wiping a glass with a towel.

Silas leaned over the bar. "Hello, Johnny. How are you doing today?"

Johnny held the glass up, inspecting it for spots. Evidently not satisfied, he continued polishing. "Good."

"Glad to hear it." Silas turned to me while pointing at Johnny. "Johnny here has always been one of my best sources of information. He hears everything about everything and knows more about what goes on around here than anyone in town. Ain't that right, Johnny?"

The barkeep shrugged.

"Johnny, I'm working on a story about the Frye brothers. You know, how they killed two men that day right here in the saloon, one of them a deputy."

"I remember that day." Johnny pointed to a table in the center of the room. "Happened right there."

Silas nodded. "That's right. Which one of them did the shooting?"

"Cleatus shot the man outside and Rastus killed the deputy."

"Yes, yes, that's the way I remember it too. They high tailed it out of here that day and haven't been back since. Isn't that right?"

"That's right. Sheriff Cahill from here in Harrisonville has been looking for them and I hear the U.S. Marshals would like to bring them in too."

"Do you know why they haven't been caught?"

Johnny grinned. "Them Frye boys are pretty smart. They spend their time around a settlement called Shoalsburgh, but any time the law gets close they scamper over to the Cherokee Nation in Indian Territory. The law don't go down there."

Silas pulled a silver dollar from his pocket and pushed it across the counter. "Thanks, Johnny, that helps a lot." He motioned with his head for us to leave.

I followed him out and stood under the veranda as the rain continued to pound the roof. He leaned his head close to my ear.

"Is that what you needed?"

"Absolutely. I don't know how to thank you."

He waved his hand in front of his face. "My pleasure, but those men are killers, you be careful."

"I will, thanks.

He raised his eyebrows. "And if you live through it, come back and tell me the story. After all, I've got a dollar invested in you now."

Taking that as a hint, I pulled a dollar from my pocket and held it out.

He shook his head. "It's on me, but I want to know how it all ends." He reached out. "Deal?"

I shook his hand with appreciation. "Deal."

I led my horse to the livery stable and made arrangements for him to stay in a stall and me in the loft for the night. I lay on my back with my fingers interlaced behind my head. I'd get to Shoalsburgh, then I'd have to figure out how to find the men. I knew I'd recognize Cleatus if I chanced to see him on the street, but I was less certain about Rastus.

Shoalsburgh, Missouri consisted of a gristmill built on Shoal Creek, two saloons, one nothing more than an open-sided canvas tent under a generous walnut tree, a general store and a combination livery stable and blacksmith shop. My teaching from Curley about observation had become so ingrained in me that I no longer had to think about it.

I smiled to myself, thinking that when I met the men I sought, I would meet them armed with more than the rifle in my scabbard. I'd been taught, first by Ma, then Curley. Others too, had played their part in my life, Mr. Grunwald teaching me that everything had its place, and Mrs. Grunwald dismissing my protests each morning as she sent me to school. I clucked to myself, appreciative of people in my life who'd taken the time to show me how a man should act. I suppose I was growing up, for I realized that by myself, I was inadequate, nothing more than a scared kid with a hope, but the teaching I had received would, I trusted, be the difference.

I was afraid, but not paralyzed, and my thoughts turned to the old soldier and his chance visit to the store that day. I jerked in the saddle, abruptly chuckling at a rapid realization. It had not been a chance visit. I laughed out loud and slapped my thigh, shaking my head at the obvious. Mr. Smithson had set that up. I thought I'd been so secretive, that nobody could see my fear, but he knew me better than anyone alive and at that moment, I could see it plain as day. I took a deep breath and mumbled, "Thank you, Mr. Smithson."

As I rode into the small settlement, I thought it odd that the Frye brothers would choose such a sparsely populated place to hide. I pulled up at the tent saloon and leaned down to look inside. Four men gathered around what looked to be the remains of an old wagon bed, but I didn't recognize any of them, so I pushed on.

I rode past the blacksmith shop, looking inside to the smithy who stopped beating on his anvil to stare at me. I assumed they didn't get many travelers through Shoalsburgh and frowned at the realization of the disadvantage that would be to me. I would be noticed as a stranger wherever I went, and a stranger asking questions in a small town would not be well received. What I needed was to blend in, and the only way I could think of to do that was to have a reason to stay long enough to find the brothers or learn that they'd moved on. And what better reason to stay than to have a job.

I congratulated myself on my brilliance and rode directly to the general store. I strolled up the steps and opened the door to the sound of the bell tinkling above my head. The storeman, thin and balding, came from the back.

"Afternoon."

I smiled my best I-can-be-trusted smile. "And to you." I took a moment to glance around the store. It wasn't as large as Mr. Smithson's, but it was crammed full of everything a man on the frontier could want. "Nice place you have here."

To my dismay, his expression didn't change at the compliment.

"Something I can help you with?"

"I'm heading west to make my fortune, but I need to resupply. You wouldn't happen to need some help would you?" It was a spur of the moment story that sounded thin as it came out of my mouth.

He shook his head. "Ain't enough business here to feed me, let alone to pay somebody else."

His tone was friendlier than I'd expected, and that gave me hope. "I see. Anybody else in town need a hand for a while?"

He stepped closer and pointed toward the creek. "You might try at the mill."

I turned to see the tall, whitewashed structure through the window. "I'll try that, thanks."

I had to backtrack through town to the main bridge to cross the fast-moving creek. Tall trees thickly covered in leafy vines lined the creek bank and were only slightly less prominent into the countryside. Someone had cleared the trees directly around the mill and as I walked to it, I marveled at the huge waterwheel turning slowly at the side of the building. I'd never seen a mill before and the workings interested me.

A large, wagon door remained closed but a smaller door to the side was propped open to take advantage of the breeze. I strolled through, stopping to watch the oversized, wooden gears turning the six-foot-wide millstones, the bottom stone one way, and the top, another. Flour collected at the perimeter then flowed into a bin at the other side of the building.

On a ledge at the top of the building, a man peered down at me. He waved, then climbed down three alternating sets of ladders to the main floor where I waited.

"Howdy."

I waved my arm. "Quite a setup." I had to speak loudly to be heard over the creaking and groaning of the gears.

He smiled. "Yes, it is. Designed it myself."

I was duly impressed. I'd always had respect for men who could build something. I leaned in again, deciding to use the same approach I'd used in the store. "I'm heading west but I'm out of provisions. I hear you might be looking for a man to work for a time."

He stood straight, then motioned to the door. He led the way and I followed outside, across a grassy area to a nearby shade tree from which cicadas chirped pleasantly. He stopped and turned.

"Sorry, I couldn't quite understand what you said."

"I said I'm heading west to make my fortune, but I need supplies. I heard you might be looking to hire a man."

I was taller than he, but he looked me up and down, then smiled as though he was pleased.

"I do need a man to drive for me. Can you handle a team?"

"Yes, sir. Grew up on a farm." I almost said in Kansas but caught myself. Kansans and Missourians weren't exactly on speaking terms that close to the war, what with the marauders from both sides exacting their vengeance.

"I'll need you to deliver flour to wherever it needs to go, even into the Nation when called for. Can you do that?"

"Yes, sir." A driving job was the best I could have hoped for because it would give me a chance to meet people from the countryside and listen for any clue I could use. I grinned inwardly because he spoke of the Cherokee Nation as though it was dangerous. In truth, that was exactly where I wanted to go if that's where the Frye brothers were hiding.

"You'll take care of the horses, sack the flour and load and unload the wagon."

"Yes, sir. You won't be sorry."

"I better not be." He pointed to the big building. "There's a room under the mill that you can stay in and you can take your meals with me and the missus. I'm John Reding. What's your name?"

"Branson Hawk, sir."

Chapter 15

The days turned to weeks and the weeks to months. The job with Mr. Reding allowed me to drive his team and wagon all over Southwestern Missouri, Southeastern Kansas and into the Nation. The trips were long and the country open with no one about, which gave me ample opportunity to practice with the rifle. I became the store's best customer, spending most of my earnings on box after box of ammunition. I practiced because I wanted to have the confidence that I would need to face the outlaws. The brothers were probably ten years older than me and much more experienced when it came to killing. For the upper hand to fall to me, I needed an edge, and I did all I could to gain the advantage, which included nightly trips to the woods to get familiar with moving in the darkness through the trees. Night after night I slipped silently through the thick groves, learning to feel my way by instinct and not solely on vision.

With the practice, I grew more confident in my ability, but less confident that I would find the Fryes in Shoalsburgh.

Three months into my stay, I was ready to move on because I hadn't heard or seen anything of them. Each week I told myself that staying longer would be fruitless, but each week saw me staying for one more in case the men showed up.

With winter in full force at the four-month mark, I'd given up. If the men were anywhere around that part of the country, I would surely have seen or heard something. My deliveries for the day were finished, so after taking care of the horses, I washed up for supper and hurried in the cold wind to Mr. and Mrs. Reding's home close to the mill. I knocked on the door and waited until I heard the pleasant "Come on in" from her.

I sat at the table, not knowing exactly how to tell them I was leaving. I'd grown very fond of them during my stay and was confident they felt the same way. They knew that my stay was to have been temporary, but the thought of leaving brought a familiar heaviness to my chest.

Before I could announce my plans to leave, Mr. Reding turned to his wife.

"You'll never guess who I saw today."

She glanced up and patted her mouth with a cloth napkin. "Who?"

"Rastus Frye."

I took a quick breath, sucking a spoonful of soup down my throat and partially into my lungs. I doubled over in a coughing fit with my napkin held to my mouth.

Mrs. Reding vigorously slapped my back until the coughing subsided and I was able to lean back in my chair. I had known Mr. Reding was not a slave owner but he was a Confederate sympathizer. He'd mentioned it several times thinking I was also a Missouri boy. But to learn in that instant that the mobbers were acquaintances of his was more than I expected. I dabbed at my eyes with the napkin.

She looked into my face. "Are you all right?"

I rubbed my mouth. "Yes, ma'am. Sorry."

They went about their eating, seemingly forgetting the mention of one of the men I'd been searching for. It took all my doing, but I held back the urge to ask the question that seared my brain. I decided that the best option for me would be for them to bring up the topic again on their own without any help from me.

Mrs. Reding placed her spoon to the dish with a small clank, then wiped her mouth and looked at her husband. I leaned forward, hoping she would ask about Rastus, but I was disappointed. She only asked if he'd been able to grease the wheels of their buggy.

Mr. Reding, in a much less delicate manner than his wife, wiped his mouth with his sleeve. "I did." He grinned. "It'll be ready for you to take to Sunday meeting."

The name Rastus Frye didn't come up again in conversation and I knew I couldn't come out and ask them. If Mr. Reding had seen the man in Shoalsburgh, I'd have to find him by myself.

My heart pounded in my chest. I had stayed those extra weeks and it had paid off. With effort, I kept my breathing normal and thought of the bartender in Harrisonville. He'd obviously been right, the Fryes had undoubtedly been in hiding in Indian country where no law could reach them, but they were in Missouri now, possibly only a few hundred yards from where I sat. I used the napkin to wipe the sweat from my brow and lip. The room, pleasant only a few minutes earlier, had become hot and the banked fire seemed to be directing all its heat to me. I tugged at my collar, then stood to go.

"Thank you for supper, Mrs. Reding." My voice was shaky and I hoped they would think it was because of the coughing fit. I didn't know what connection they had with the Frye brothers and at that point I didn't care. There would soon be death in Shoalsburgh in the very near future, possibly mine, but I hoped that would not be the case. I felt the fear, but didn't despise it. All I could do was move forward with the end in sight.

Dark was nearly upon me as the next day I returned from a delivery and glanced over to see two horses grazing on leftover grass inside a corral at the old Montgomery place. A shiver ran down my back as I stared. The horses hadn't been there earlier and I concluded that it was more than coincidence. The Fryes, at least Rastus and more than likely, Cleatus also, had been seen in town and suddenly two horses appeared at an abandoned cabin?

My fingers itched for the feel of my rifle, and if I'd known for certain that it was the Frye brothers, I would have gone straightaway to finish what I'd come for. I slapped the reins on the big draft horses and made them step lively to the Reding barn where I hung the harness on the pegs and turned the horses to the corral. I took time to feed them, then, with rifle in the crook of my arm, I walked to the house in the increasing darkness to see Mr. Reding.

The half-moon cast eerie shadows from the trees as I approached the house. I felt the weight of my rifle with satisfaction. It was like an old friend and I knew it wouldn't let me down. I unconsciously rubbed the barrel, then stopped at the porch and checked to make sure it was fully loaded. Satisfied, I pulled my coat more closely to my shoulders and knocked on the back door.

Before an answer came from inside, I heard a noise from the woodpile. I turned to see Mr. Reding striding toward me with an armful of wood.

"Hello, Branson. Delivery go all right?"

"Yes, sir." I pointed upstream. "Saw some horses at the old Montgomery place?"

He nodded. "That's the Frye brothers. I saw Rastus yesterday. Didn't hardly recognize him with his beard and long hair." He motioned for me to open the back door of the house so he could enter. "Come on in for supper."

I shook my head. I hoped the Frye brothers weren't his friends, because by the time this night was over, he'd have two less friends. "Thanks, but I'm not hungry."

He looked at me, then shrugged and entered. I pulled the door closed behind him and took a deep breath before walking up the road and turning on the overgrown path that led to the cabin. I stopped at the tree line and could see the front of the cabin was treeless with the exception of two large trees on either side of the door. There was a thick covering of grass over the ground on the less-than-an-acre clearing which was surrounded by thick, dense trees running along the creek and only slightly less dense farther away.

I waited, concealed behind the thick trunk of a tree and studied the cabin. There were no windows and the door was closed, but the two horses continued their grazing, so I was reasonably certain the Frye brothers were inside.

I cupped my hand to my mouth. "Cleatus Frye, are you in there?"

Call it what you will, possibly stubborn pride or even downright stupidity, but I wanted the brothers to know who I was and why I was there, and I concentrated on Cleatus specifically because Jacob had said he only had nine fingers so I knew he was the one who'd shot Ma. I suppose it might have made more sense to sneak to the cabin, knock on the door and start blasting at the first opportunity, but that was not for me. I'd seen this moment countless times in my dreams, and in those dreams, I'd seen the fear on their faces when they realized the time had come to pay for their deeds and I was there to extract payment.

I hollered again. "I know you're in there, Cleatus. You've had your fun and now it's time to pay."

The door opened slightly. "Who are you and what do you want?"

"Name is Branson Hawk. Say it to yourself over and over. I want that name on your lips when you take your last breath."

A rifle barrel jutted from the door and several shots came my direction, one hitting the tree I stood behind. I raised my rifle for a shot but the door closed too quickly. I concluded that the slight opening of the door had less to do with letting his voice carry as it did with trying to pinpoint my voice. Interesting, I thought, that I could be learning in the middle of the fight.

I pressed harder. "You're trapped in there, Cleatus. I've a mind to set fire to the cabin and let you burn. It would serve you right 'cause that's what you did to my brother and sister." I ran ten steps to my right in case they decided to open the door and shoot again.

The door cracked but no rifle appeared. "You've got the wrong men. Come on in and let's talk about it."

I shook my head at the ploy. "I don't think so. We've crossed paths more than once. Remember the deputy in Harrisonville?"

The rifle pushed out again and another volley of shots scattered into the woods, but this time I was ready and fired two shots into the crack at the door. The men were well hidden so I had no expectation that I'd hit one of them, but of a certain, they would be more cautious.

"All right, we're coming out with our hands up. Don't shoot."

The sliver of light escaping the crack suddenly grew as the door swung open wide, but instead of coming out with their hands up, they bolted through the door shooting their rifles from the hip as fast as they could work the levers. One ran right and the other left to hide behind the trees on either side of the door. None of the shots they had fired were particularly close to me, which enabled me to raise my rifle to be ready to shoot. I concentrated on the man on the right. The light from the door clearly showed him as he crouched behind the tree.

He raised his rifle, pointed my direction and fired one shot. Idiotic fool. He had no idea where he was shooting, but I could see him plainly in the light. I squeezed the trigger and saw him fall back against the cabin, then stagger away from the protection of the tree and fall to the dirt.

"Rastus?"

The call came from the second tree a fraction of a second before a barrage of shots thudded into the tree behind which I stood. I concluded that Cleatus must have seen the flash from the muzzle of my gun to determine my position. One man was dead, but I realized I now faced a seasoned adversary. I would have to use every skill Curley had taught me if I hoped to survive the night.

I retreated into the trees and slowly moved southeast because I knew Cleatus would make a dash to the safety of the trees beyond the clearing. It was the most logical option, get to the trees and escape under their cover. The other option was to attempt to cross the creek, and only a fool would jump into the icy water and hope to run to safety before freezing to death.

I moved silently through the trees, stopping periodically to listen for any movement from him. It was only by chance that I heard the scraping of a branch against his clothes. I stopped and listened, surprised that he'd already moved more deeply into the trees and I handn't seen or heard. I cursed my negligence, then rushed to keep up with the fleeing man.

I hurried through the trees, running parallel and stopping occasionally to listen, straining my ears for any sound to tell me where he was, but I was disappointed each time. Cleatus was a woodsman, better than I had expected. I would have to be as good as I'd ever been. I silently thanked Curley for teaching me to embrace the darkness, and it was only using the skills learned from many nights of practice that allowed me to dodge silently through the trees to keep pace with Cleatus, at least where I thought he was. In my mind I went over the layout of the woods. We were fast approaching the clearing around the mill. If I could get there first, I'd have a clear field of fire.

I reached the treeline where I stopped and waited. I was almost certain I'd overtaken him, and suspected that he, like me, looked through the moonlit clearing to the mill building. I brought my rifle to my shoulder, ready for when he bolted into the clearing to make a run for it, but as I waited and the fast-moving clouds obscured the moon, I grew less confident that he was where I'd expected.

I faded back into the trees and stealthily moved toward the creek to be close to where I thought he might be hiding. It was a dangerous tactic and I knew it, but I had no choice because if he escaped, my chances of finding him again were nonexistent. I moved slowly, careful not to rub against any brush and not to step on anything that might cause a sound. My hope was to get close then go to ground and listen for any movement from him. I finally reached a place where I dared not go farther in case he waited for me. In the distance, I could hear the gurgling of the creek and I tilted my head back and forth, ears trying to pick up any sound out of the ordinary. I determined I'd wait. He had to be close.

I nearly jumped out of my skin when I heard him merely ten yards from me and I could only assume he'd slipped through the woods like a ghost. He obviously didn't know I was there when he, deciding to take a chance, jumped and ran for the clearing. I ran also, but by the time I reached the treeline I saw the last flash of a flannel shirt disappear through the small door into the building.

I took several deep breaths, filling my lungs with the cold, winter air. He was inside and with the wagon door closed, I knew there was no other way out. With rifle at the ready, I moved closer to the creek to come up on the corner of the building. I stopped only long enough to lift the gate to allow water into the waterwheel sluice. It groaned in protestation, but as the water rushed through, the big wheel slowly turned, then picked up speed as its momentum grew.

I hurried to the small door into which he'd disappeared. It remained open so I leaned against the wood of the wall knowing with its thickness, no bullet could penetrate.

The large gears complained in their moving and the millstones turned, one against the other causing a terrible noise. I knew the building well, but he didn't. In truth, that was the reason I'd opened the water gate. He would have to pay close attention to the moving parts inside the tall room. Any distraction for him meant less attention on me.

I leaned toward the door. "I know you're in there, Frye."

Two bullets hit the inner wall in rapid succession and I felt relief that my estimation of the thickness of the wood had been correct. I visualized the inside of the mill and guessed at his location from the sound to the gunshots, but a guess was the best I could do because of the echo of the shots and the noise inside the building.

"Your brother's dead, Cleatus."

I edged as close to the door as I dared and waited for an answer that would tell me where he was, but he chose to remain silent.

I glanced toward Mr. Reding's house, hoping that he hadn't heard the squealing of the mill or the shots and felt the need to investigate, but with the trees between the mill and his house, the sounds did not carry far. I saw no lights so I turned back to the door.

"My name is Branson Hawk. I want to hear you say it." I had decided to badger him, to rile him and wait for a mistake. "You're all alone now with no brother to look out for you." I paused, waiting, listening. "Do you hear me? Branson Hawk. I want you to remember that name."

He chose not to speak, but I heard the familiar clack of the lowest ladder. I'd heard that sound countless times while working in the mill when Mr. Reding would climb to make adjustments. Two bolts at the bottom of the ladder were loose and when he climbed past the midway point, the ladder would shift and cause a sound loud enough to be heard.

I knew where Cleatus was and it made sense. There was no way out, except possibly the windows high above the gears. I rushed through the door, understanding that as he climbed, at least one hand would have to stay on the ladder. The interior of the large room was dark with only a shaft of moonlight coming through an open window at the top of the building, but it was enough for me to see him clearly. He turned quickly and one-handed, took a shot, but it missed badly because of his lack of control.

I stood from my crouched position, suddenly aware that with only one free hand, he could not work the rifle's lever. He leaned out and stared at me as he came to the same conclusion. His leaning brought his face into the shaft of moonlight and I saw his light colored hair.

"Your brother's dead, Cleatus, and you're next."

"Who are you?"

"I told you. My name is Branson Hawk from Lawrence, Kansas. You killed my family."

His voice rose in fright. "It wasn't me. You've got the wrong man."

I shook my head. "Don't think so." I stepped away from the wall and held my rifle on him. One pull of the trigger was all it would take. "How many fingers do you have, Cleatus?"

In desperation, he screamed and the unexpectedness of his move surprised me. With catlike quickness, he jumped from the ladder and turned in midair with both hands on his gun. He dropped toward the hardwood floor while working the lever to take a shot.

I fired once and the force of the bullet turned him a quarter turn, then without firing a shot, he hit the floor with a loud noise. I waited, but he lay still and unmoving. With a new round in the chamber and gun at the ready, I walked to his side, seeing his rifle on the boards nearby. It had a shattered stock caused by my bullet and I realized I'd hit the rifle instead of him. I kicked it away, then held my gun firmly against his chest.

He lay on his back in shallow, labored breathing, glaring at me with hate. I saw no wound, at least no hole from my bullet because he'd been protected by the stock of his rifle, but he had nothing to protect him now.

"You've killed your last victim." I pushed the gun harder against his chest and he grunted at the pain. I'll admit that I had no reservation about hurting him because of all the pain he'd caused me. For an instant, I thought of gut-shooting him and letting him suffer an agonizing death. It would serve him right.

He raised his hands in surrender and I could plainly see the little finger of his left hand was gone at the knuckle. The idea of gut-shooting him grew. He deserved to die a miserable death and I would be happy to bring him to his end.

"Do you remember how you lost that finger?"

He didn't answer but only looked at me. The terror in his eyes was gone. I supposed he had come to the knowledge that he had only minutes to live.

I leaned down, hissing the words. "My Ma done that. I hope it hurt for a long time." My finger tightened on the trigger, but a noise at the door distracted me and I heard a voice.

"Don't pull that trigger."

I looked and saw a man enter the building, and as I watched, several more men with rifles and torches came in to stand nearby. Their torches lit the room and eerie shadows danced on the floor.

I looked to Cleatus before returning my gaze to the new

men. "He deserves to die."

The lead man held his hands up. "That may be, but if you shoot him, it will be murder plain and simple."

"There's only one thing plain and simple about it. He killed my family and I'm going to kill him."

With hands still up, the man stepped forward and I saw for the first time, a badge on his chest.

"Who are you?"

"Deputy U.S. Marshal Nathan Hayes. If that is Cleatus Frye you're holding down with that rifle, we've come to take him in. I've been on his trail since the war ended. He'll be tried for the crimes he's committed. If found guilty, he'll either hang or be sent to prison for a long time."

"Why don't I kill him and save y'all the trouble?"

Marshal Hayes lowered his hands and took a deep breath. "Because I don't think you are a murderer. If you pull that trigger, you won't be any better than him."

I looked at Cleatus and gritted my teeth as I recognized the truth of the marshal's statement. As much as I wanted it to be otherwise, I could see he was correct, but the battle raged in my mind. I didn't particularly care at that moment that I'd be no better than the killer under my gun. I wanted with my whole soul to pull the trigger and send him to his grave, but a vision of my Ma flashed into my brain. Her blue eyes stared at me and she slowly shook her head.

I sighed as the tenseness of my shoulders relaxed. I slowly released my finger from the trigger and glanced at the marshal. "You'll make sure he pays for what he's done?"

"We will."

I lowered my head. "Then take him and be gone before I change my mind."

Four men rushed forward. When they surrounded him, I stepped back, carefully lowered the hammer on my rifle and watched them roll him to his stomach. With little gentleness, they put irons on his hands and legs, then pulled him to his feet and led him, shuffling and limping, out the door and into the clearing beyond.

Marshal Hayes waited until the men were gone. He held a torch and he walked to me, holding the light and looking into my face. He sucked air into the side of his mouth. "How old are you, son?"

I lowered the rifle to rest on the floor while I held the barrel. Exhaustion settled over my shoulders and into my chest. My quest was over, there was nothing more. All I wanted to do was lean against the wall and rest. I breathed deeply. "Coming eighteen, sir."

He grasped my arm and led me out the door and away from the noise. "Did you say eighteen?"

"Yes, sir."

"Why were you chasing Cleatus Frye?"

"Him and his brother killed my family back in Kansas at the start of the war."

He whistled low. "And you've been chasing him since?"

I shook my head. "Only for the last six months or so. I tracked him here to Shoalsburgh. I learned tonight that they were holed up in a cabin up the creek from here." I pointed north. Cleatus ran here to the mill and took cover. This is where it ended."

"Well, you done us a favor. We heard he might show up in Shoalsburgh. We were camped down the creek and when we heard the shots, we came a runnin'." He looked toward the mill building and cocked his head. "Where are the rest of y'all?"

"Rest?"

"Yes, the men who helped you?"

"Other than folks who gave me clues and taught me what I needed to know, nobody helped me."

His eyes opened wide. "You cornered him all by your lonesome?"

"Yes, sir."

He whistled again. "Good grief, boy. We've had half the U.S. Marshals in Missouri trying to track him down, and you're telling me you did it all alone?"

I shrugged.

"And the brother, Rastus?"

I pointed north again. "At the cabin, dead, but it wasn't murder. He was shooting at me."

He nodded. "Figured as much." He lifted the torch and looked at me again. "Coming eighteen."

It wasn't a question, but more of a statement. I answered anyway. "Yes, sir."

He cocked his head and looked to the mill building one last time before turning to me. "Have you ever thought about becoming a U.S. Deputy Marshal? We need good men like you." He motioned ahead, inviting me to walk with him. "How about you ride back to Springfield with us and meet the marshal in charge?"

I hadn't thought of what I'd do when my quest was complete. I had nowhere else to go so I nodded. He clapped me on my back and together we strode into the night.

Epilog

I cringed on my knees on the dirt of the abandoned livery stable and contemplated my last breath when the booming sound of a gunshot echoed in my ears and I felt myself falling from my kneeling position. Strange, I thought, I'd felt no pain. Then I somehow realized that a brain shot through the eye would be instant death, so no pain should have been expected.

I hit the ground and felt my head bounce on the hard dirt, then I thought I heard a smaller gun, a closer gun, firing rapidly amongst retreating footsteps. That was the last thing I heard before a thick darkness pressed at me from all sides.

Sometime in the darkness, the sound of conversation reached my ears, but it sounded distant. I pressed my eyes closed, trying to drown out the sound, but had no luck. As I breathed, I felt something holding my chest, squeezing me, not allowing me to breathe deeply. My confusion was complete. I was certain I heard footsteps approaching, then a hand touched my shoulder.

My eyes seemed sealed closed, but with tremendous

effort, I was able to open one barely enough for a stream of light to enter. The pain was immediate. I squeezed again, holding my eyes tightly closed. Where was I?

"Hawk?"

I heard the voice but made no attempt to answer. All I wanted to do was drift back to where I'd been a few minutes earlier. The place with no pain, no light and no sound.

"Hawk. Can you hear me?" The hand on my shoulder pressed harder.

I heard but didn't care. My chest ached and I could scarcely breathe, I probably couldn't have answered if I'd wanted to. I wiggled my fingers. If only I could rub the grit from my eyes, then I'd feel better.

Another voice, slightly farther away, drifted into my consciousness. "He's barely alive. The shot would have killed any normal man."

The first man answered. "But he's no normal man, he's Branson Hawk."

The mention of my name was startling. They'd been talking about me! I raised my eyebrows and with all my might tried to pull my eyelids open so I could see. Two thin slivers of painful light crashed against the backs of my eyes. I blinked, closing my eyelids tightly, then in slow degrees, opening them again. Slowly, my eyes adjusted to the glare and when the image grew clearer, I saw Colonel Marcomb grinning down at me.

I licked my lips. They were so dry. I felt like I could drink a gallon of water. I tried to speak but my voice was nothing more than a croak.

He touched my shoulder again. "Don't you be trying to talk. The doc here has been wanting to get you measured for a casket, but I wouldn't let him. You had us worried. It's good to see you back."

Back? Back from where? I tried to remember, but everything seemed a blur and nothing made sense. I licked my lips again. "What happened?"

"That friend of yours wasn't much of a friend. Do you remember I warned you against going in there alone?"

My recollection was cloudy and I couldn't quite gather in the missing pieces. Friend? What friend? Somewhere in my brain I had thoughts of the old livery barn, but nothing more.

"Well, after you left, I decided I'd tag along with the scattergun to make sure you would be all right. When I heard the shot, I ran to the door and saw him kneeling next to you with his pistol in your eye. I couldn't shoot him without hittin' you, so I sent one barrel over your heads. I've never seen a man so quick. He was up and running faster than lightning, turning and shooting toward me as he ran. Before I could pull the second trigger, he jumped into one of the stalls and ducked through a hole in the outside wall to the alley."

The pain in my chest flared in sudden remembrance. I gritted my teeth and swallowed. I'd made a stupid mistake, one that had almost killed me. Curley had taught me better than that. What had I been thinking? I blinked again, holding my eyes closed for a time while the recollection came rushing back. In my memory, I saw the man purposefully waiting to draw. He'd wanted me to know that he was faster and wasn't worried about my puny attempt with my pistol, and he'd proved it with calculated ease. I had proven my ability with a six-gun many times, but with a sinking feeling, I realized that I was far from the gunman I'd made myself up to be. I frowned with sudden self-doubt. Would I be good enough to take him when I found him, for find him I must. It had been my quest once, and it would be again.

I opened my eyes and whispered, "Thanks for saving my life."

He shrugged and pointed to his left. "When I saw you

were hit hard, I ran to get the doc. He said you likely wouldn't make it, but you proved him wrong." He looked back to me. "Who was the man, anyway?"

"Cleatus Frye." I paused, blinking heavily. "He killed my family when I was a kid. I hunted him down long years ago and turned him over to the U.S. Marshals in Missouri. I thought he was still in prison."

Marcomb rubbed his fingers along his jaw line. "Well, he's obviously not in prison any longer."

He turned as if to go, but I reached to grasp his wrist. "My next assignment... ." My strength was gone, but I had to make the request.

He shook his head. "There won't be any assignments for you for a while. You need to concentrate on getting well."

I squeezed his forearm. "I'm going after him."

Marcomb tapped a tooth with his fingernail and slowly nodded. "When you get well enough, I'll sign your orders."

I released his wrist and let my arm fall back to the bed. I would get well and I would practice with my .45 more than I'd ever practiced before. I would find him and I would take him if it was the last thing I did. And, contrary to what I'd told Curley all those years earlier, I would enjoy watching Cleatus Frye draw his last breath.

The End

Author's side notes that might be of interest:

Bushwhackers in Kansas and Missouri wreaked havoc on both sides of the border prior to and during the Civil War. Pro-slavery raiders brought death and destruction to eastern Kansas while abolitionist Jayhawkers did the same to western Missouri.

Killings, burnings and lootings became so prevalent that eastern Kansas became known as Bleeding Kansas during that time. Lawrence was one of the hardest hit cities, having been destroyed once in what became known as the Sacking of Lawrence in 1856, then again when Quantrill's raiders attacked in August of 1863.

John S. Reding built a gristmill on Shoal Creek and the resulting settlement became known for a time as Shoalsburgh, Missouri. It is now known as Redings Mill.

The area known as the Cherokee Nation in what is now northeastern Oklahoma was frequented by outlaws because there was no extradition until it, along with the designated Indian Territories to the west, became the Oklahoma Territory.

No small number of Quantrill's raiders became outlaws immediately following the Civil War. Some of the more notable ones were: Jesse and Frank James, Jim and Cole Younger, and Archie Clement to name just a few.

Other books by Randall Dale
Pardner's Trust Series:
Pardner's Trust, Cowboy Up
Friends in Deed

Hidden Regrets
A Good Man Gone

Branson Hawk, U.S. Marshal Series:
The Wichita Connection
Dead Man's Gold
The Beginning

The Captain's Coat
The Posse

Manufactured by Amazon.ca
Bolton, ON

20006110R00136